THE LIVING REALM

ALSO BY JORDAN TANNAHILL

FICTION

The Listeners

Liminal

PLAYS

Prince Faggot

Is My Microphone On?

Declarations

Botticelli in the Fire

Sunday in Sodom

Concord Floral

Late Company

Age of Minority: Three Solo Plays

THE LIVING REALM

JORDAN TANNAHILL

4th ESTATE • *London*

4th Estate
An imprint of HarperCollins*Publishers*
1 London Bridge Street
London SE1 9GF

www.4thestate.co.uk

HarperCollins*Publishers*
Macken House, 39/40 Mayor Street Upper
Dublin 1, D01 C9W8, Ireland

First published in Great Britain in 2026 by 4th Estate

First published in the United States by Farrar, Straus and Giroux in 2026

1

A catalogue record for this book is available from the British Library

ISBN 978-0-00-879454-5 (hardback)
ISBN 978-0-00-879455-2 (trade paperback)

Designed by Gretchen Achilles

Printed and bound in the UK using 100% Renewable Electricity at CPI Group (UK) Ltd]

FSC
www.fsc.org
MIX
Paper | Supporting responsible forestry
FSC® C013604

In all the world there has never been, there is not, and there will never be any such thing as time. There is only place. What people call time is only place after place. Eternity is here already, and it has no mystery about it; eternity is just another name for this endless scenery where we wander from one place to another.

—GERALD MURNANE, "First Love"

THE LIVING REALM

It had been Europe's worst drought in twenty generations, but Teufelssee did not lose its water. As the Earth baked like a hot stone, the lake remained, even as the continent's mightiest rivers ran dry and yielded their secrets. In Spain, the village of Aceredo resurfaced after having lain submerged below the River Lima since the creation of a great reservoir in the early nineties. On the dusty basin of Lake Como, a hundred-thousand-year-old skull of a deer was revealed, alongside the bones of hyenas, lions, and rhinos, while in Lombardy, Bronze Age timber foundations appeared on the cracked-earth floor of the River Oglio. Scattered across the riverbed of the Danube lay the remains of Nazi battleships, like corpses resting in the positions in which they fell. All season we suffered under an unrelenting white sky, bright and airless, but still, we swam at Teufelssee. As the shorelines receded across the continent, the hunger stones appeared, carved with their dire pronouncements, *Wenn du mich siehst, dann weine*, a warning to us future generations of the coming famine to be endured now that the waters had once again sunk to these levels. You will suffer as we once suffered—"*If you see me, then weep,*" Birgit murmured, as she read of the battleships on her phone, her hand held to her brow to block the midday sun falling on our blanket. I found it startling, the ease by which the ghosts of our collective past could so easily emerge from their places of hiding, as if time itself had simply evaporated in a single heat wave.

Teufelssee had never once lost its water in the centuries since humans had begun keeping records of such things. What was a century to a lake, though, but a flicker of light? Teufelssee belonged to deep time, geological time, a great shard of ice calved from the tongue of a retreating glacier, left to slowly melt, carving a kettle-hole into the substrata two hectares in area, with no inflow or outflow, no stream, no aquifer, the meltwater gradually replaced by twenty thousand years of rain. The lake was now a sanctuary for herons and cranes, and the nude bathers who visited throughout the summer, reclining on their blankets and towels in the sloping meadow along the southern bank, hidden deep within the Grunewald, the forest that lay at the edge of Berlin like its shadow. My waterproof Timex once slipped from my wrist as I ventured out into the middle of the lake with Birgit, and however much I fumbled after it, the watch sank from my grasp, down past schools of unbothered bitterlings. For years after,

I would imagine the digital numbers counting with diligence the passage of seconds, minutes, hours in the cold dark. This summer Gabor, Birgit, and I took near-daily refuge at Teufelssee, a summer that was singular not only for the drought but for a series of strange and unaccountable occurrences at the lake to which I alone seemed to bear witness.

Birgit was the reason I first moved to Berlin back in 1991, a week shy of my thirty-fourth birthday, she having selected me over dozens of other postdoctoral candidates for a newly created fellowship with the Freie Universität's archaeology department. Not only had she arranged my work visa, which was far from easy to do in those days, she secured me my flat near the university, where I have continued to live these past three decades, the second floor of a subdivided turn-of-the-century house which I grew to love, despite the stifling heat, small windows, and regular concussing of my head against the sloping ceilings. At Cambridge, I had gone to some lengths to keep my sexuality private from my colleagues, lest it prejudice my chances for advancement. My performance of male heterosexuality, whenever it had been required of me, involved my adopting an affect of disinterest; I simply pretended to be slightly less enthusiastic about everything. Upon my arrival in Berlin, however, I felt no need to hide anything of myself, nor my wonder, from Birgit, a bull dyke with a peroxide buzz cut who ran fisting workshops on Friday nights with her girlfriend, Antje, in gay bars and bathhouses. The couple taught gay men the techniques they had long refined on one another—balling, finger blooming, double-handed slip-sliding—in an effort to decenter the phallus as the focus of sexual gratification. Amid the AIDS epidemic, it was their belief that the community needed survival strategies that increased rather than precluded pleasure. "I can either sit holding hands in hospital rooms, or I can show my friends how to put them to use and maybe save some lives," Birgit told me during my first week at the university. While I never attended the Freitags Fisting Club myself, the workshops had apparently, on more than one occasion, attracted unsuspecting amateur boxers who turned up expecting something very different, and in some cases stayed anyway.

Gabor had himself been a competitive boxer and weight lifter while a student in Budapest, and would tell anyone who asked, and often those who didn't, that he was living in exile in Germany after being hounded out of Hungary by its nationalist president, Viktor Orbán. Gabor's long-running feud with Orbán was both highly public and deeply personal. They had been grammar school classmates in their hometown of Székesfehérvár, and had both received scholarships to study abroad from liberal billionaire philanthropist George Soros, who later founded the Central European University in Budapest at which Gabor had taught cultural theory. As Orbán's politics took a turn to the far right, his former benefactor and mentor Soros became his bête noire. Orbán claimed the Central European University was intentionally fomenting dissent and inculcating Hungarian youth with depraved, foreign ideologies like gender theory, and went on to target a number of academics in the press, including Gabor, with whom he had longstanding animosity from their boyhood days. Gabor had resolved to stay in Budapest and fight, but after the windows of his flat were smashed, and his door spray-painted with the words *gonosz buzi*, evil faggot, he resigned himself to decamping to Berlin, where he took up an appointment at the Freie Universität, his office facing into the same courtyard as Birgit's and mine.

On a preternaturally warm evening this June, Gabor and I walked our bicycles toward the sand-swept forest that borders the lake, where generations of men have wandered the great hypostyle hall of conifers in search of sex. We walked in twilight until we reached the pine glades still possessed by the phantoms of men, and joined ourselves to their namelessness, our hands and knees rutting in the dirt, fingertips gripping dark soil, the smell of the earth, of excrement and semen, alkaline and glistening on thighs, on palms, on backs. Not more than a dozen yards away, a sounder of wild boars, insatiable and whiskered, snorted and sauntered past in the underbrush. I eventually extricated myself from the scrimmage, wiping myself clean with a fern frond before deciding to set off down a path that I seldom took. I ventured deeper into the forest than I normally strayed, walking for a time without spotting anyone. The path gradually narrowed, until it tapered off into a grove of ferns, some of which reached as high as my waist. I was just about to double back when I noticed a young man in the mid-distance leaning against a tree, head shaved, eyebrows so blond as to appear nonexistent, a face that was half cherub, half pug, naked save for a pair of jean shorts and gray sneakers. He was a carbon copy of Lukas, exactly as Lukas had looked thirty years ago in the prime of his life, and for several seconds I was overcome by this powerful irruption from the past. The man did not notice me at first, and the longer I observed this stranger, the less convinced I was that he was a stranger at all, looking as I was at a body that I had long ago memorized, every hair, every mole. I wanted to call out to him, but found I could not. I willed myself to move, to take a step toward him, just one, and then another, and as I approached the man through the fern grove, he finally glanced in my direction, and looked at me with Lukas's same heavy-lidded gaze. He then turned slowly, and disappeared from view behind the tree on which he'd been leaning, as if suggesting I might follow him. When I reached the tree, however, he was gone. I searched for him, wandering the forest for the better part of an hour, and though I encountered other men, some fully clothed, some astride fallen logs stroking their erections, some in tight clusters being serviced by unseen supplicants, I never did find the mysterious man who bore such an uncanny resemblance to my dead lover. When I finally reconnected with Gabor in the central clearing and told him of the disorienting experience, he shrugged and joked that it would be far from the last time a handsome man would elude me in that forest. "Only rarely does what we seek, seek us in return," Gabor said, "and thank goodness for that."

Gabor had once said to me that he believed cruising was the arena in which we best applied our tens of thousands of years of evolution as hunter-gatherers. I think a part of me was drawn to cruising for very much the same reasons other men loved to fish, less so for the catch itself than for the discrete rewards of patience, for the many long minutes of waiting spent in stillness, feeling time dissolve into place. It was about the careful observation of a landscape and the gradual accumulation, over many years, of a knowledge of that landscape; to know that in a certain grove, at a certain hour, on certain days of the year, men would congregate, or that if a man disappeared down a particular path, what the chances were that he would reappear in one or another clearing. One came to learn the intricate variations of eye contact, sustained and averted, how to distinguish an accidental brushing-past versus intentional contact, what was an invitation, and what was a rejection, how many times men would do a full tour of the paths before they decided to settle for who was there, and how likely they were to settle for you.

The cruising grounds lay at the foot of a large hill called Teufelsberg, both lake and hill bearing the name of the Devil, Teufel, and as I walked my bike down the sandy path out of the glade, I could see the hill looming up in silhouette against the fading light. Teufelsberg, though innocuous enough in appearance, was built entirely from the ruins of firebombed Berlin: churches, apartments, banks, shops, schools, centuries of life and of loss, all of it jumbled together in a great rubble heap and sodded over to become the highest point in the city. In the early days of the Cold War, the Americans built a listening station atop the hill, its ears trained on East Berlin, and farther too, deep beyond the Iron Curtain, tracking the movement of tanks and the flight paths of aircraft. As I walked my bike, I could just make out the dark forms of the geodesic radomes, sprouting like giant spores from the derelict surveillance complex. From the top of Teufelsberg, one could gaze out over the dark expanse of the Grunewald, the waters of the Havel and Wannsee, and the city splayed out to the horizon. Since the fall of the Wall, the listening station at Teufelsberg had become yet another urban ruin reclaimed by copper thieves, adolescents, birds, nesting mammals, the weather.

While biking home, I reflected on my encounter with Lukas's doppelgänger, and it all began to feel rather unremarkable. People constantly looked like one another, I was near-daily struck by such resemblances, yet I marveled at the strength of feeling the sighting had stirred in me. As I biked, I realized that it had been years since I had last thought of Lukas, and I smiled recalling our first fateful meeting in those very woods, not long after I had arrived in Berlin on fellowship in 1991. In those first months in Berlin, I had heard rumors of a lake where men cruised deep within the Grunewald, and after considerable effort, having been pointed in contradicting directions by locals I passed along the paths, I eventually found the shoreside meadow dotted with nude sunbathers of all ages, and spent the rest of the day among them, stripping bare and dipping in and out of the cool water and my book, before venturing at last into the nearby forest in search of the rumored cruising grounds. Unfortunately, as much as I wandered, twigs snapping underfoot and scraping my shins, I did not encounter a single soul, and would later learn not only that I was in an entirely wrong part of the forest, but that it was virtually impossible to find the right grove had one not been led there by the previously initiated. With the sun now well below the tree line, desires thwarted, I returned to the meadow to find my blanket and knapsack missing. It took me a long moment of searching before I could admit to myself that my belongings had, in fact, been stolen, and another moment to take stock of just how desperate my situation was. In the front pocket of my knapsack I had left my wallet and keys, but most crucially, I had stuffed all my clothes and shoes into the body of the bag. I was completely naked in the middle of the darkening forest, a half hour from the nearest S-Bahn stop, and kilometers from my flat. I marveled at the depths of my stupidity. To make matters worse, while searching for my knapsack, I had let the last group of sunbathers leave the meadow, paying no heed to the direction of their departure, and so was now fully and truly alone. The thief could have at least left me my blanket to wrap myself in, I thought, as I sat there in the grass hugging my knees to my chest. As a pasty, protestant Mancunian, it had been enough for me to strip naked among strangers, but the prospect of now having to wander nude down a public path toward the city, then another twenty minutes through busy intersections and down residential streets to my flat, was beyond what I could bear. I began playing scenarios in my head of my arrest, the revocation of my fellowship, the unraveling of my career. I considered staying the night and waiting for tomorrow's first sunbathers to assist me, but no, that was madness, I had to stand, I had to begin walking, and I would simply explain my dilemma to the first person I encountered along the path, and hope that my rudimentary German and their reserves of empathy were sufficient enough to avoid catastrophe. And so I stood, my spindly body ghostlike in the dusk, and I began walking up the slope toward the footpath, and, upon reaching it, stepped barefoot onto the remarkably painful gravel. I imagined myself a mystic walking over burning coals, and this helped distract me for a time, until I felt myself illuminated from behind by the approaching light of a cyclist, my shadow elongating before me, and I swiveled around and began waving, but the cyclist did not slow, instead blowing past me without so much as turning his head in my direction. A laugh escaped me, imagining the cyclist thinking that the gays were becoming markedly more brazen of late. I walked for what felt like half an hour without encountering anyone, the gravel beneath my feet eventually giving way to sand, until I noticed a dark form emerging from an adjoining path up ahead. The figure of a man stepped onto my route without noticing me, and began walking in the same direction I was headed. I called out to him, and then whistled, for the distance between us was considerable, which caused the man to stop, and turn, and suddenly emboldened I began running toward him while calling out an explanation in my limited German. By the time I was close enough to see the man's face, I was out of breath, and as I attempted my explanation again, in a calmer, quieter manner, he cut me off to say that he understood. He looked to be all of twenty-three or -four, a young man of striking beauty wearing an industrial safety pin through his ear, baggy jeans, and a flannel shirt, which he proceeded to remove and tie around my waist. "There, a nice skirt for you," he said in German with a chuckle, his dark, loamy musk reaching me as he crossed his arms in his white undershirt, before adding that he would walk with me to my bicycle. When I admitted to not having one, he looked at me more confounded than he had at my nakedness. "What are you doing here without a bicycle?" he asked, sounding almost irritated. I told him I lived in Dahlem, not so far from the southern edge of the forest, and after another skeptical look, he begrudgingly assented to walking me at least as far as Clayallee. As we walked, I noticed the flannel shirt around my waist had the same stale-piss smell I recognized from riding beside other unlaundered punks on the U-Bahn. In the end, Lukas, as he introduced himself, walked with me all the way to my flat, and I was heckled only twice by passing cars. Still, I knew the night's ultimate abasement was yet to come, the moment in which, upon arriving home, I would have to ring the bell of the ground-floor flat to summon my formidable landlady, Mrs. Bauer, to unlock my front door.

"I—I can't speak to her like this," I said to Lukas, gesturing to my barely concealed nakedness as we turned down my street.

"Okay, Mr. Bean, leave it to me," he said, placing his hand on my shoulder. Lukas had informed me on our walk that I reminded him of the hapless Rowan Atkinson character, newly popular even in Germany, and this association only added to my general state of mortification.

"And say what, what are you going to—"

"Hey—relax. I'll just explain that you were mugged while sucking dick in the forest." Lukas, it seemed, liked to serve up his jokes cold and unadorned by so much as a smile.

As I stood a respectable distance back, half hidden in shadow, Lukas rang Mrs. Bauer's doorbell, and just as I began to despair that she was sound asleep, the door opened to reveal her wiry, goaty frame backlit by the harsh, uncovered bulb of her entryway. A rat-a-tat exchange in German followed, her eyes darting between Lukas and me, before she threw up her hand, and batted it in my direction, while muttering what I assumed were curses upon my descendants, or perhaps she was mourning her sorry luck to have survived the war only to be stuck in her widowhood dealing with the ludicrous antics of homosexuals. The entire ordeal had been so consummately humiliating that, upon entering my flat, and bidding good night to Mrs. Bauer, whose scowl merely deepened in reply, I assumed there was not a drop of eroticism left to wring from the night, but to my surprise I was wrong, and after Lukas fucked me on my couch and coffee table, I held him gently as we stood in the warm baptism of my shower.

Some thirty years later, freshly in her nineties, Mrs. Bauer was still my landlady, having increased my rent by only €440 over that time, and though her daughter Lisbeth helped her with groceries twice a week, and her son-in-law looked after repairs to my flat when needed, Mrs. Bauer remained sharp and self-sufficient. Thankfully our relationship had warmed a considerable degree over the years since that fateful night. As it happened, while I was mounting the staircase to my flat, having arrived home from cruising with Gabor, my thoughts consumed by Lukas and his doppelgänger, Mrs. Bauer opened her door and called to me.

She needed help with changing the light bulb in her entryway, still uncovered after all of these years, for she was no longer steady enough to use the stepladder she kept in her front closet. After I made the replacement we exchanged a few words about the heat, and the car attack on Kurfürstendamm that week, and what little I had been doing with my retirement, before I bade her good night.

As I walked into my flat, I put on Bartók's Piano Concertos Nos. 1–3, performed by Géza Anda and the Deutsches Symphonie-Orchester Berlin, conducted perhaps a tad too strenuously in places by Ferenc Fricsay, poured a brandy into a snifter, and then myself into an armchair. I texted Gabor that I had arrived home safely, and he replied the same, and joked that he hoped for my sake I did not reencounter Lukas's double while cruising in the future, as anything other than the real thing was sure to be a disappointment. I closed my eyes and sat there, at once in my flat and also in the upper mezzanine of the Berlin Philharmonie, beside Lukas, whom I had brought to see the symphony on our second meeting, as thanks for my nocturnal rescue. It was during the intermission, as we stood drinks in hand, that Lukas asked what had brought me to Berlin, and in my halting German, I told him of my fellowship. My research at the time was focused on a cave called Hohle Fels in the Swabian Jura, which had been inhabited by successive waves of Upper Palaeolithic peoples over many millennia. When the cave was first crudely excavated in the 1870s, the bones of long-extinct cave bears and mammoths were discovered, before being largely forgotten about. Archaeologists returned in the mid–twentieth century, and began a series of digs in which they found primate stone tools, mostly crafted from Jura horn stone. Lukas nodded as I spoke, his brow furrowed, I wasn't sure how much he was following, but I pressed on, telling him that, in a month's time, I would be setting out for the cave with my team to begin work on a sequence of layers belonging to the Aurignacian culture. Without a moment's hesitation, he asked whether he could join me, and I laughed, but he was serious, and told me he needed out of the city for a time. He had recently been let go from his job as a line cook at a restaurant in Mitte, frequented by politicians and diplomats, and knew how to prepare food for large numbers, and could cook for my crew. (What he failed to tell me at the time was that he had lost that job of a year and half after he and another line cook were caught adding drops of LSD to the soups of six members of the Bundestag from the Christian Democratic Union.) He promised me that he would work hard, and I smiled, telling him I would think about it.

This was the first fieldwork of my fellowship, my reputation was riding on it, and I wanted to prove myself deserving of all the work Birgit had gone to in bringing me to Berlin. Instead, I all but destroyed my standing in her eyes. In the days leading up to the dig, there was still much that needed to be sorted—generators, work tents, ground transportation from Stuttgart, portable toilets—and virtually all of it had started falling to her. I began taking a full day to return her phone calls, and was in the office half as much as I should have been. My sorry excuse was that I had become completely infatuated. I felt stricken with it like an illness. I began spending most nights with Lukas, which meant spending most mornings in some state of recovery. He took me to parties at the semi-derelict squat where he lived, a kind of pirate's lair with its crumbling walls draped with flags and banners, where I encountered his truly dire housemates, hunched, gremlining in the corners, vacant eyes, dried crusted blood around their nostrils; I had to remind myself that they were still kids, twenty-two, twenty-three, and they might find their way yet. He gave me my first communion of ecstasy, a blue pressed pill on my tongue in a dark corner of Tresor, the old bank vault of the demolished Wertheim Department Store, where sweat dripped from the low concrete ceiling and where I kissed Lukas for an hour beside a speaker that shook our breath. I am sure I had those nights to thank for the tinnitus I became aware of years later while lying awake at night, one of the many ways Lukas continued to haunt my body. To the extent that Lukas was even aware of it, his beauty seemed like something of a minor annoyance to him, something he put up with rather than celebrated or attempted to preserve, but it persisted despite his casual sabotage of bad haircuts and his general disinterest in grooming. Lukas had been an aspiring writer, though doubted himself, and always refused to show me the fragments of prose I would catch him working on. He once exploded in a kind of adolescent rage as he emerged from the shower to find me peeking at a page of his notebook, which, from what I could tell, was nothing more than a rather straightforward diary entry. He loved to slip the names of great writers into conversation, Genet, Duras, Mann, though I was never entirely sure whether he had actually read them. He was a fixture in the city's underground scene and moved along the periphery of its burgeoning art world, posing for sculptors and painters, something of an accidental muse who secretly aspired to be a creator in his own right. Lukas was once photographed at Teufelssee by a friend along the lake's shorefront path, in a fallen ash tree, its branches leafless and dead, but sustaining several new trunks of fully formed living ash trees, to such an extent that it was not entirely clear whether they were all one tree or several, or if the original tree could even be considered dead when it continued to live through the other trunks. Lukas, scrawny, naked, head shaved, was perched on the bough of this simultaneously living and dead ash, its silver leaves clattering like a million tambourine cymbals in the wind, his look pensive, brooding, like a feral child caught on camera by an anthropologist. In a second photograph, Lukas sat on the tree's bough as a young woman he'd met raving the previous night stood on the bough contrapposto holding on to the trunk. This second photograph always recalled to my mind Cranach the Elder's painting *Cupid Complaining to Venus*, in the position and placement of the pale figures against the dark, dense foliage of a Germanic forest. Many years later, long after Lukas was dead, I would have the uncanny experience of attending a major museum retrospective of the photographer's, walking into the gift shop, and finding this photograph of Lukas emblazoned on mugs, T-shirts, notebooks, and fridge magnets.

Birgit was not impressed, to put it mildly, when she discovered the cook I had hired for our dig was also my lover, the very one who had been so preoccupying my attention. On our second day at Hohle Fels, glancing out from the canteen tent at the improvised kitchen we had set up behind it, she saw him peck me on the cheek as I helped wash the lunch dishes.

"Who the hell is he?" she asked me with barely

concealed rage, the cigarettes between our fingers being the pretext for our private chat. "Did you pick him off the street?" I asked her to keep her voice down, Lukas was within earshot, and she lowered her voice to a whisper somehow even more fearsome. "I can't believe you invited this boy you're fucking to our dig—"

"He's an experienced chef, we needed a cook—"

"Oh, an experienced chef, I see, and was that lunch some of the Michelin-star cuisine we can expect moving forward?"

"I admit the lunch was disappointing, but I told him to work within a budget."

"What's disappointing is how you've let this boy completely play you. It's pathetic. Or maybe it's me who's been played."

"Birgit—"

"You know what I'm about, I'm not some *prude*, for fuck's sake, and I'm sure you're having your mind blown a bit in Berlin, and your dick too, I'm very happy for you, but keep your dick out of my dig—understood?"

Thoroughly chastened, and with a healthy fear of Birgit, I began giving Lukas a wider berth around camp, and working late into the night to make up for my earlier state of distraction, though I couldn't quite bring myself to send him packing (in part because I had already paid him in full). At Hohle Fels our team from the Freie Universität was collaborating with a group of postgraduate students from the University of Tübingen. All of us were in our twenties and thirties, and all of us were in heat. Sounds of furtive masturbation and frantic couplings in tents could often be heard throughout the night, and by the second week the shower trailer reeked of semen. The sun beat down on us with such unforgiving intensity that our clothes would be sodden by midday, beads of sweat dripping from our noses onto the worktable in the canvas tent as we catalogued artifacts. Lukas walked around the camp with a musk so potent it felt theatrical. When Lukas wasn't in the kitchen, he would sometimes join us at the dig site, where he would help with some of the menial but laborious work like clearing earth, and sandbagging. Despite Birgit's initial anger, over the proceeding weeks Lukas became her preferred company on her smoke breaks. Watching them together, I came to realize that they shared a humor in their native tongue that excluded me, and always would. Lukas and I sought to maintain an illusion of propriety for the better part of a month, but eventually, after realizing we were fooling no one, he moved his sleeping bag and belongings into my tent. That summer was among the happiest of my life, the ache of the dig in our muscles by evening, swimming in the Ach to clear the dust from our skin, before nights spent exploring Lukas's body with the day's same patient eye to discovery. The piglet-pink of his eyelids. The near-invisible swirl of white-blond hairs on his ass. The hidden scar on his upper thigh. With the soft brush of my tongue, I excavated his body. One night I whispered to the darkness that I would give up the rest of my life to live just five years as Lukas's lover.

While neither Birgit nor I would have admitted as much to others, there was a shared sense between us that the dig had been something of a disappointment, until one fateful morning in our final week, when two post-docs from Tübingen and I found six small mammoth-ivory fragments lodged in the basal deposit, which we gingerly cleaned, and laid out onto a piece of white paper on the worktable. Over several hours, with the aid of tweezers and a magnifying lamp, we carefully assembled the fragments into a six-centimeter figurine of a headless woman. The entire team crowded into the tent, knowing we had found something remarkable, and it was in those first jostling moments of jubilation that Birgit dubbed the figurine the Venus of Hohle Fels. Finding our Venus within the Vb layer of the Aurignacian sequence placed her age between thirty-five thousand and forty thousand years, making her the earliest example of expressly human figurative art found anywhere on Earth. Our discoveries at Hohle Fels successfully pushed back the age of known non-stationary human figuration by nearly five thousand years, and were heralded in archaeological circles, but amid the global upheavals that year there was little in the way of broader public notice, it certainly didn't see us rendered in statuary or our names carved in stone, in fact it barely got a half-page notice in the university's student newspaper.

Ever the by-product of Germanic pragmatism, Birgit was as disinclined to believe my story about Lukas's doppelgänger as Gabor was, and knowing this, I didn't raise the matter again with either of them. The frequency of our visits to Teufelssee increased throughout the month of June, driven as much by the rising heat as it was by my private curiosity and desire to re-encounter the man who so resembled my dead lover. If Birgit and Gabor were aware of this ulterior motive, they were gracious enough not to let on. One afternoon we were mid-conversation on our blanket, in our usual spot in the meadow, when the shrieks of children drew our attention to the forest's edge. We watched as a wild boar and her three piglets sauntered out from a nearby copse of birch, tawny-coated, with gray faces, bristled snouts, and tiny eyes like black tourmaline. "There's our girl," Gabor said with a smile. This was our first sighting of Elsa all season; she was a fixture at the lake, beloved by the longtime regulars like ourselves, her name somehow known by many but of mysterious origin, though Gabor liked to claim she was named after the fashion designer and aristocrat Elsa Schiaparelli. The piglets must have been from her spring litter, and were no doubt desperate from the drought, cleaving close to their mother as they rummaged through the plastic wrappers and beer bottles scattered around the base of the nearby garbage barrel. As they ventured farther into the open, a few yelping sunbathers scattered, and we watched as Elsa suddenly absconded with the laptop bag of an elderly nudist, who gave chase across the clearing to peals of laughter from around the meadow. With jowls and genitals bouncing, the chuckling nudist reclaimed his bag at the forest's edge, waving good-humoredly to the clapping onlookers.

After this flurry of excitement, Gabor pulled a perspiring bottle of Müller-Thurgau from his cooler bag, and as he uncorked it, he recounted how, for the past couple of weeks, his neighbors in Zehlendorf were perplexed as to why their flip-flops and running shoes were disappearing from their gardens at night. He had become implicated in the mystery when he noticed his pink Crocs were no longer on his back patio where he was sure he had left them. "I thought maybe we had an avid fetishist in the neighborhood," he said, characteristically deadpan, while filling three small plastic cups with wine. Finally, earlier that morning, while Gabor was taking out the trash, he spotted a young fox slipping through a hole in a nearby fence with a plush blue slipper in its mouth, and he followed the thief into a nearby abandoned lot, where hidden in the overgrowth was a collection of nearly a hundred sneakers, sandals, boots, and high heels.

"A hundred!"

"The reincarnation of Imelda Marcos herself," Gabor said with a little flourish of his hand.

In the early evening, the three of us walked into the forest and sat for a time in the sun-dappled clearing where men reclined on blankets alone and in pairs, their bikes resting against nearby trees. Piles of charcoal dotted the glade, the remains of campfires from weekend parties, which police had begun issuing warnings about during the drought. The forest had no garbage bins, being a natural conservation site, and revelers had been leaving piles of trash strewn about instead of portering it home. These parties, which had grown in popularity over lockdown, when young people desperately sought a place to commune, had started to cause friction with regulars (ourselves included), who had cruised the woods for years and feared the added scrutiny from authorities. The garbage also brought more wasps, several of which presently whirred near us. The men in the clearing periodically looked up from their books to watch whoever entered the warren of paths branching off into the forest, and, if enticed, would wait a respectable minute before rising from their blanket and setting off in the same direction, usually naked save for their sneakers. At one point, Birgit seemed to be catching the eye of a mulleted trans boy who circled back into our sight line not once but twice, the second time being confirmation that it was indeed Birgit he was eyeing, and after some gentle coaxing from Gabor and me, she took her cue to follow at a distance into the brush. Gabor had already arranged an assignation for later that evening with two leather daddies on holiday from Marseille, and so departed not long after. Once I was alone, my thoughts naturally drifted to Lukas, and I scanned the forest's edge with the faint hope that I might spot the man who had so preoccupied me these past couple of weeks.

Instead, after a couple of minutes, I noticed Thomas, one of the forest's regulars, walking his bike into the clearing, and after we met eyes I waved him over to where I sat. Thomas and I had briefly been lovers in the early 2000s; he was a respected mycologist, and once told me that for every step I took within the forest there were roughly three hundred miles of fungi beneath my foot, every mycelium with more networks than my brain had neural pathways. As we sat together on my blanket, we spoke of the parties, and the warnings, and the fear they would invite more police presence, and he then told me how, in 1950, his uncle had been part of a huge roundup of a hundred men caught frequenting Frankfurt cruising spots patrolled by undercover police. "He lost his job, his marriage, and was dead six years later from cirrhosis of the liver." Thomas told me the Stasis had been preoccupied with monitoring cruising, and that he had recently been shown a Stasi map of Prenzlauer Berg, by a friend at the Schwules Museum, dotted with color-coded markers identifying various locales of gay life within the district. The map was dominated by red dots, which were buildings where at least one gay person was known to have lived, and which, as Thomas recalled, appeared to be about on every block in the area. The green dots, the second-most plentiful, were bars known to be welcoming to homosexuals. And finally, there was a single black dot, which Thomas said was identified as an "Internationally Known Public Toilet," which made me laugh.

"The Stasi files did have their own peculiar sense of humor," he said, smiling and shaking his head.

We fell into an easy silence, before he turned to me and gave me a look of such simple tenderness, a look that did not seem to expect anything in return, only to merely acknowledge the fact of my company, and the years that had passed between us. The clearing had begun to fill with the most astonishing golden light, and, knowing that within an hour the sun would dip below the tree line and the area would cool and fall into shadow, Thomas rose from the blanket, stretched, and announced his intention to discover what awaited him in the woods. He picked up his bicycle, and with a coy smile and a raised hand goodbye, he set out across the clearing and disappeared into the undergrowth on the far side. As much as I had wanted to join Thomas on his foray, I was now the guardian of Birgit's bike, and so I waited there dutifully, savoring the warm glow, until she returned twenty or so minutes later with a full recap, both of us taking up our bicycles and setting off toward her flat in Wilmersdorf for dinner.

Two days later, I stepped from my shower to find my phone ringing beside the bathroom sink. It was Gabor, calling in distress to ask whether I had heard the news about Thomas. I felt my chest tighten, and replied that I hadn't. While scrolling Facebook that morning, Gabor said he had begun seeing obituaries posted and shared by mutual friends, and learned that Thomas had died suddenly in his sleep of a stroke on Tuesday night, and was discovered by his sister the following morning. Well, that was simply not possible, I interjected, as I had seen Thomas at Teufelssee on Wednesday evening, and had spent nearly an hour talking with him before biking to Birgit's. Gabor was silent for a moment, and then replied that no, the post from Thomas's sister clearly stated Tuesday night as his time of death, the discovery being made the following morning, and surely she of all people would not be mistaken, but I insisted I had sat speaking with Thomas on Wednesday evening, and then biked directly with Birgit to her flat. "Was your threesome with the Frenchmen not Wednesday evening?" I asked Gabor, and he confirmed it had been, but that nevertheless I must be misremembering. This disagreement around timing almost eclipsed the shock I felt at the news, which hit me in full after I hung up. Though my time with Thomas had always been sporadic, of late only a handful of hours a summer, I felt genuinely bereft. His family held a private memorial to which I was not invited.

While reading the news at my kitchen table a couple of mornings later, I was astonished to come upon a photo of Elsa the boar on the BBC, dashing across the meadow at Teufelssee with the laptop bag in her mouth, pursued by the elderly nudist with blurred genitals. Opening the article, I read a tongue-in-cheek account of the incident that I had frankly all but forgotten, my thoughts being so preoccupied with Thomas's passing.

Embedded in the article was an eleven-second video of the hapless man giving chase as onlookers yipped and hollered, myself somewhere among them. Someone had evidently recorded the would-be heist and posted it to Twitter, where it had immediately gone viral, racking up over a million views. Several other news outlets had picked up the story, if you could even call it that, and "Berlin boar" was now a trending topic.

"Absolutely outrageous," Gabor muttered to Birgit and me as we searched for a new spot to lay our blanket later that afternoon, arriving at Teufelssee to find it completely overrun with people.

"Do you reckon they're here because of Elsa?" I asked.

"What other explanation could there be? I've never seen it so busy, and it's a cloudy weekday."

"What are they hoping to see? There's no way she's going to come when there's this many people."

To my surprise, however, a couple of hours later, as the three of us lay reading our books, we heard voices erupt in exclamation and, turning, saw Elsa and her piglets emerging from the forest near the trash barrel. We then watched as the foraging pigs were encircled by a group of tourists proffering snacks while simultaneously filming on their phones. It was clear the presence of so many people rattled Elsa but especially her boarlets, who were acting more skittish and erratic than usual, dashing away from their mother at times, halfway to the forest's edge, before charging back to the trash barrel, a kind of strange and agitated loop. Gabor rose from our blanket, and began clapping his hands loudly in the direction of the clustering tourists while shrilly whistling and accosting them in German, causing them to startle and turn, and for Elsa to scamper back into the woods with her brood. "They're wild animals, you fucking idiots," Gabor grumbled as he returned to our blanket.

Not twenty minutes later, a green golf cart pulled up along the upper path, and the three of us watched as a man in a forestry office shirt climbed out, and began his descent into the meadow. Gabor and Birgit rose to their feet to intercept him, and at a distance beyond earshot I watched as they greeted the man, gestured toward the trash barrel, and explained what had just unfolded. After a brief back-and-forth, I saw Birgit's face become very grave, and on their return to the blanket, both she and Gabor looked crestfallen, explaining that the official was the newly appointed director of the local forestry office, and that he had just informed them that Elsa and her offspring would be destroyed as a matter of priority. The boars were becoming too used to humans, he claimed, too accustomed to being fed human food, and while they were only an occasional nuisance for the time being, who was to know what diseases they carried, or when the mother might grow more aggressive. I was surprised by the strength of my own feeling at this news. Those of us who knew Elsa had grown fond of the cheeky sow, and the suggestion that she should be culled despite having shared her living space with us for years felt like a cruel injustice. It was hardly her fault that she had become an overnight celebrity; why should she and her children be the ones punished for our collective idiocy? I suggested, perhaps impetuously, that we might start a petition on Elsa's behalf, and Gabor looked at me from the tops of his eyes. "For a pig?"

"Why not?"

"I'm just saying, there are many causes."

"Well. What's wrong with a small cause?"

The small cause for which both Gabor and Birgit were keener for my attention, however, was that of my own psyche. My mind was troubled by my encounters with Thomas and Lukas's double, and by something else as well, but what it was exactly I could not quite seem to grasp. After a night of particularly disturbed dreams, I woke just before five in the morning, and, knowing I would not fall back asleep, I walked into the kitchen and lit the burner beneath the stovetop espresso maker. After my coffee, I set out from my flat, before the first joggers and dog-walkers, as the first U-Bahn trains departed their stations to begin their routes below the city, the white fluorescent streetlamps blinking off one by one in dawn's light. I was walking, I realized, as if by instinct, back into the dark of the Grunewald.

The Grunewald had long occupied an outsized place on the dark edge of the city's imagination. For Lukas, the forest was not only a zone of personal liberation but a staging ground for the city's libidinal unconscious. In the years when we were closest, he became fascinated by the story of the Wild-frei, marauding gangs of adolescent boys orphaned in the Great War, their faces painted like pirates and their bare chests scrawled with obscene tattoos, who during the Weimar lived deep within the forest's recesses. They had been working-class boys, boys in the Wandervögel hiking clubs who had strayed off the path and underwent a brutal initiation, a knife fight that, if survived, would be followed by sado-sexual rites while tied to a tree. Dressed with a flamboyant mixture of adolescent male virility and haphazard effeminacy—Chaplinesque bowlers, old women's hats adorned with ostrich plumes, garish scarves, leather shorts, long pendant earrings—they moonlighted as hustlers in the city, turning tricks in sailor bars, robbing and pleasuring the bourgeoisie, before retreating to their forest hideaways. Lukas made many attempts, all abandoned, at writing the story of an adolescent who sets off in search for his wayward older brother through the down-rent hustler bars of East Berlin, whereupon hearing rumors that his brother has joined the mysterious Wild-frei, ventures into the dark heart of the Grunewald to their hideaway, where he too is initiated into their ranks as he secretly longs to be. The story existed in many fragments, often repeated and reworked, in Lukas's notebooks, and it seemed to me that the very thing that first drew him to the story also impeded his progress with it. He spoke to me once about sharing a kind of spiritual kinship with these lost boys, who spurned the civilized world that had abandoned and abused them. Lukas himself had run away from home, and he maintained an obstinate refusal to tell me anything of his own childhood. Over the years I managed to glean a few scraps of his past—a household of three brothers in a housing block in Wedding, grandparents who lived on the other side of a curtained partition, a father who drunkenly groped the boys at night until they were old enough to break his nose. Mostly these details were shared fleetingly, half alluded to in dark jokes. Each time we ever came close to any honest conversation about his family, each time I saw what felt like a window into that part of his soul, I would draw near only to find it was a mirror, my own reflection staring back.

Entering the forest that morning, I made my way

along an old imperial bridle path, wide and grand, colonnaded by plane trees, and soon found myself approaching the Jagdschloss, a sixteenth-century hunting lodge silhouetted against the rising light. The lodge had been built by the prince-elector of Brandenburg, who with his wife, Hedwig, fell one night through the lodge's rotten floorboards into the room below, wherein Hedwig was fatally impaled on a pair of mounted antlers. In the dying days of the German Empire, the Jagdschloss had played host to a great sex scandal, when fifteen aristocrats invited at the behest of Princess Charlotte held an orgy at the lodge after which the guests were blackmailed, presumably by the princess herself, the intimate details of the evening circulated in letters, leading to denouncements, backstabbing, and ultimately, the dueling death of one Leberecht von Kotze. I had spent many hours wandering the lodge's creaking halls with Lukas, admiring its near-unrivaled collection of paintings by both Cranach the Elder and the Younger, including one of the Elder's oddly erotic renderings of Judith with the head of Holofernes. It was there, in fact, while standing in front of *Smoking Women*, a small painting by the seventeenth-century Leiden painter Jan Steen, that Lukas first told me he loved me. But that morning of my walk, I made my way past the hunting lodge as its paintings and ghosts slept, and continued onward through the woods. I entered a clearing of unruly waist-high blueberry bushes, the *heidelbeeren* coming into their full season, the berries left unpicked by local foragers due to the persistent and irrational German fear of tapeworm eggs sticking to low-hanging fruit. I walked until the pines grew amber and spindly, and limbless except at their very tops, and noticed the grayed trunk of a dead rowan scrawled by termites in a kind of Proto-Sinaitic script, its hollow, vertical cavity bivouacked by cobwebs.

After an hour, the air still cool and damp as a dog's nose, I arrived at last at Teufelssee, taking the path worn by decades of footfall through the sloping meadow to my usual spot by a thicket of goldenrod, the same place Lukas and I would often spread our blanket. At that hour, before any other visitor, the lake belonged to itself, a steely eye staring up at the vault of lifting dark. All about the lake, life renewed itself. Tongues of mist licked and flickered across its surface, which reflected the waveform of the forest. The water bugs scrawled their frantic calligraphy. A scarlet fire beetle ascended a furred blade of grass. A Eurasian siskin chirruped from the lowest bough of a pin oak, joining its voice to the chorus of goldcrests, nightingales, blackcaps, marsh tits, bramblings, fieldfares, redwings, and chaffinches. I watched as a black stork with its crimson beak perched on a log half submerged in the shallows, a log I had often sat on while summoning the resolve to submerge my body in the bracing water. How might I witness what time was actually doing, I wondered, and not what I assumed it to be doing as I raced about my life? I resolved that I would spend my day at the lake and, with patience, might catch sight of what I was only half sure I was looking for.

Over the next several hours, the lake's first visitors began to arrive. An elderly couple with two large striped umbrellas took up their spot in the upper meadow, the woman with pendulous breasts and her compact husband both smoking fat Cuban cigars, their radio softly playing local news. The dreadlocked *soixante-huitard* with her tutu and Doc Martens took up her spot by the fallen log, and was joined soon after by two families with small children. The kids were the first into the water, splashing naked after minnows in the lake's shallow cove. A lanky, bearded man with rimless glasses took up his place not far from mine, released a monumental uncut penis and untamed bush from his white briefs, and began sketching the shoreline in his notebook with charcoal pencils. A group of friends in their twenties set out their blankets, three of them with massive, floppy straw hats, two with top-surgery scars, all six stick-and-poked, and began passing around supermarket prosecco, Club-Mate, and keys of ketamine. I listened to their joyful, scattered conversation for a while—Eurovision, fascism, ADHD—until

Vincenzo, Andrea, and Tommaso appeared. This venerable trio of bronzed, leather-skinned Italian queens in their seventies were as close to Teufelssee royalty as it came. They sat hunched on a sprawling orange throw in the tall grass to the left side of the clearing with no view of the water whatsoever, which to me always begged the question of why they bothered coming to a lake at all, but they had their shaded corner and they were territorial about it, to the point where I had witnessed them ask a cuddling young couple to relocate so that they could take up their preordained spot. The Italian dames sat on their orange throw holding their books but never reading, instead alternating between fierce, rapid-fire arguments in Piedmontese, and silently glowering at the other visitors. I knew that one of them was the former general manager of the Milanese Opera, another was a pilot for Alitalia before its bankruptcy, and the third worked as an archivist for the Gemäldegalerie, but I was ashamed to admit that I could not remember which was Vincenzo, which was Andrea, and which was Tommaso, and I had known them for far too many years to ask for clarification.

From my spot in the meadow, I had a clear view of Teufelsberg rising above the tree line, crowned with its decaying geodesic radomes. The specter of the abandoned listening station looming over the lake, the nude sunbathers, the cruising forest, made me consider the ways in which we observed one another, and in our constant watching and listening sought to understand how we were supposed to be. I realized I came to Teufelssee not so much to swim, or sunbathe, or escape the heat, but to glean fragments of conversation from adjacent blankets, to watch the young mother holding aloft her baby's arms as he danced in the sparkling shallows, to savor the careless virility of a young man loping like a dog from the brush having just relieved himself, for how else could I know how to live if I did not watch others in their attempts? Life was an act of mirroring, just as Baudelaire once wrote of the flaneur, *we might liken him to a mirror as vast as the crowd itself,* and on that late June afternoon I felt myself as vast as Teufelssee, and all the bodies it held along its sloping, grassy banks. There was something beyond joy or idle leisure, something closer to worship, in that kind of bearing witness, in observing the ways time played upon nature, and the bodies of others.

I was reminded of a photograph I saw many years ago, taken the summer of 1892, of Henry Scott Tuke painting a nude man *en plein air* for his canvas *A Woodland Bather,* the mustached Tuke a man of thirty-five at that point, fully dressed and long-sleeved despite the season, his tawny-haired muse a decade or so younger, ruddy-faced and rosy-eared, with an aquiline nose, emerging from the forest onto a rocky shore, and I had been struck while looking at the photograph by the parallax of observing a man in his prime beholding a yet younger man, observing Tuke meditating on the gulf of time that lay between them, his awareness of something his young muse could not yet apprehend, that the endless summer would one day draw to a close, our limbs kissed by the sun only a handful of days, so many fewer than we had once thought, and each of them ever shorter. After some searching I found the photograph on my phone, and as I regarded it again, after so many years, it occurred to me for the first time to consider the presence of the absent photographer, perhaps a friend or lover of Tuke's, another link in this chain of witnessing and desire and myself, at once the oldest and youngest witness, looking back on youth, but also on the dead, and in so doing seeing both past and future at once. I had a moment's thought that I might turn around and see yet another man beholding me beholding the photographer, the painter, the muse, and who, I wondered, would this future witness be, and who his witness, and so forth. The sensation this induced in me was not Aschenbach's longing on a Venetian beach but something more akin to a kind of Whitmanesque exaltation of being suspended in time, all of us idling together on the rocky shore of this lake at the edge of the woodland, witnessing and being witnessed by one another, for eternity.

I returned to the lake to reencounter myself, the many selves I had been on its shores over time like so many discarded snakeskins, just as I became the pentimenti of my past desires when I reentered, naked, the nearby woods, seeking to rejoin the pleasures that lingered behind every bush and fallen trunk. What if every man I had ever cruised in the forest waited just around the next bend, like a half-glimpsed phantom? Perhaps I too had never left. In a world in such violent flux, I could not think of anything that remained as unchanging as Teufelssee, I could not imagine one feature of Berlin that had changed less in a millennium than this lake, and perhaps it was this constancy that I sought more than anything, this constancy that reminded me of my own mortal pace, somewhere between that of a skylark and a linden, the constancy that gave the lake the illusion that anything lost to time, our youth, our loves, might be dived for and retrieved from its depths with great enough effort.

Rising finally from my blanket rather stiffly, I set off toward the shaded cove along the shoreline, where I dipped a foot into the water, then the other. Wading with gradual acclimation to my waist, I steeled myself for a moment before leaping into the lake's chilly embrace. I swam a wide arch around the young people on the pontoon raft moored at the lake's center, smiling at their antics, some sort of backflipping competition, and opted instead for the quiet of the lake's far side. As I reached the white buoys dotting the perimeter, I turned my head toward a stretch of beach secluded from the meadow, and noticed a pale man sitting with his knees in his arms, his toes touching the water's edge. As if sensing my gaze, the man held his hand to his forehead, and, looking in my direction, grinned in a lazy, sun-drunk way that seemed so familiar to me, and in that instant it felt as if my blood had suddenly been replaced with the thermocline of the lake's bottom—it was Sebastian, in broad daylight, the same age he had been when I had last seen him boarding a train to Regensburg. We had only been lovers for three weeks at the time of his diagnosis. His trip to Regensburg was to be a brief visit, to break the news to his mother, but a mutual acquaintance would later tell me that he never returned, and that his mother had nursed him in his childhood bedroom until his death. I regarded his dead ringer from a distance, more than twice as far as was comfortable for conversation, the surface of the lake just below my bottom lip. In Sebastian's same unhurried way, the man rose to his feet and stretched, in full awareness of my unabashed stare, with which I could not find a single discrepancy from the body in my memory, right down to the small keloid scar above his left hip. He then brought his gaze back down to the water and began walking into the lake to a depth that slowed his pace, before diving in and disappearing below the reflected sky. I waited for him to reemerge, but he did not immediately, and I imagined he was traveling a distance underwater, perhaps all the way over to me. But as the disturbance of his dive subsided, the water remained still. I treaded in place, my heart pounding, until the sun disappeared behind clouds, and I began my return to the far shore where the meadow met the lake. I was so shaken that it was not until I was already halfway returned to my blanket that it even occurred to me to call for help. I turned and ran toward the dark green shack where visitors could rent paddleboats, though rarely did, and I shouted for a lifeguard who eventually appeared in the form of a teenage boy, not more than seventeen, stepping from the shack in a red bathing suit and looking almost annoyed at my panic. I pointed to the far end of the lake as I frantically recalled the events, and the boy seemed almost confused by the fact that he was being pressed into some form of action. After asking me several questions, the boy trilled his whistle, and called to those still swimming to return to shore, before grabbing a paddle, a fluorescent-yellow rescue board, and a life ring, and setting out into the water in the direction I had indicated, to do what, at this point, I really couldn't imagine. Was he going to dive down and try to retrieve the man? By what means? Perhaps the man had become caught on one of the submerged trees I had sometimes seen early in the year, before a season's worth of swimmers had turned up the lake's sediment and clouded the water. I scrambled back across the meadow to my blanket, rummaged through my knapsack for my phone, dialed 112, and breathlessly described the situation to the dispatcher. The three elder Italians noticed my distress, and one strode over to me, placing his hand on my shoulder while listening to my conversation. It was remarkable how consistently my German failed me in moments of agitation, and I found myself grasping for words like *Rettungsschwimmer* and *Ertrinken*. All the while, in the distance, the young Rettungsschwimmer in his red shorts continued to trill his whistle as he neared the middle of the lake on his board, clearing the last stragglers from the dock, and as people came to shore they joined the small crowd that had begun to gather, craning their necks to find the source of the commotion. Vincenzo, Andrea, and Tommaso waited with me until the ambulance arrived. No body was found that afternoon, nor was one found by the divers who combed the lake during the following two days of its closure.

Gabor accompanied me to the police station that evening so I could provide a deposition, and offered to stay with me overnight despite my suspicion that he did not believe my account. As Gabor cooked me *lecsó* in my flat, I told him of my unshakable belief that the man in the lake had in fact been Sebastian, not a look-alike but Sebastian himself, as impossible as I realized that sounded. Gabor watched with silent concern from the kitchen as I riffled in my desk drawer for the field notebook in which I was certain I had hidden a small passport-sized photograph of my dead lover. Returning eventually to the kitchen with the photograph, I recalled for Gabor the afternoon I had met Sebastian at Teufelssee in the summer of '93, and how after we had swum and dried ourselves in the sun, he led me to a hidden clearing where after we had fucked we lay next to one another talking in English about Bachmann's *Malina*, which I had brought with me to the beach that day. I smiled to remember how Sebastian had mocked my posh accent, and how defensive I became with this stranger whose name I didn't even yet know, and how I went to great lengths to explain that I was born working class, the son of an accountant and a housewife from Salford, and how any airs or affectations were aspirational in nature, driven by a college-age shame for my background which I no longer harbored. Sebastian and I were inseparable over the next three weeks, until our first big row, during which I stormed out of his flat and descended the flights of his building's staircase in the dark while he shouted down after me. We did not speak for five days—until he called to tell me he had tested positive. My sympathy was immediately clouded by a selfish terror, followed by a three-week purgatory, as long as our entire romance, in which I waited for my own results, which by a miracle came back negative. As I recounted all of this to Gabor, a heaviness returned to my chest, one that I knew well and had carried for years. Why had I not boarded that train with Sebastian? Why hadn't I found a way to write or call him? Why had I never visited him in Regensburg? There was only one simple truth, now abundantly clear—I had been a coward. Too spineless, too terrified of sickness and death to be even proximate to it, I had somehow convinced myself I had no further obligation to Sebastian, our passions having already cooled the week of his departure at the first appearance of conflict, a passing dalliance from which I had been lucky to emerge unscathed. I let myself imagine that Sebastian had eventually returned to Berlin, and was living contentedly with new lovers, perhaps a steady partner, and that the decision to let our contact lapse had been a silent and gently mutual one. I could see now, all too clearly, that it had been a heartless one, made unilaterally without a shred of compassion or grace. I felt physically ill. Gabor reached across the kitchen table and put his hand on mine, interrupting my spiraling monologue, to express, in his cautious and diplomatic way, concern for my mental state. He suggested I speak to a psychiatrist. In the end, I reassured him that I was fine to spend the night alone, and after dinner and some reluctance on his part, he left me to myself.

In the early hours of the morning I was roused from my sleep by a dull thud. It had been a quiet sound, but one my primal brain registered as not belonging to the usual nocturnal soundscape of my flat. I lay in bed for several moments waiting to hear it again. What if it had been the sound of my front door being opened? What if there was someone creeping about the flat? At some length, I summoned the resolve to throw back my covers, pull on my bathrobe, and walk into my living room, where, upon turning on the light, I saw no one. Everything was as Gabor and I had left it. Just as I turned the living room light back off I heard it again in the darkness, a muffled thump coming from somewhere below the floor, as if from a pipe, or perhaps Mrs. Bauer's flat. I debated whether to walk downstairs and knock on Mrs. Bauer's door, but it was half-five in the morning, she would still be asleep with her hearing aids out. I felt a mounting anxiety but pushed it down. To have uncertainty cast on my perceptions, to be told I could no longer trust my senses, had put me in a very strange, almost dissociative headspace. I felt sure I had heard something, just as sure as I had been about what I had seen at the lake, and yet already I felt doubt creeping in. I lit the burner below the espresso maker and then completely forgot about it as I sat at my kitchen table, replaying moment by moment the previous day's events. In the light of morning, it felt clearer to me than ever that it had been Sebastian himself who I had seen, not a doppelgänger, nor a specter, but somehow the real man displaced in time. He was no less real than I felt my hand to be as I pressed it against the tabletop. Flesh and blood and sentient—but what was he aware of, that Sebastian? What had he seen when he looked at me? Had he recognized me? And what did he understand of this game that time was playing with us? As the sun continued to rise, I tried as best I could to gather my thoughts into my notebook, and this helped calm and focus my mind for a while until, at a quarter after eight, I decided to check on Mrs. Bauer. I dressed myself, descended the small staircase to her flat, and pressed her buzzer. I waited, and after a minute I tried the buzzer again, and then a third time, but still she did not come to the door. I knocked firmly and called her name. I took out my phone, dialed her number, and listened to the faint sound of it ringing inside. After four rings I ended the call, ran up to my flat, opened the small tin box I kept on my bookshelf, and removed a spare key to Mrs. Bauer's. Dashing back downstairs, I fit the key into the lock, and with a firm turn to the right, pushed open the door.

"Mrs. Bauer?"

The flat smelled of cheap washing powder and mildew. I could see a light on at the end of a cramped hallway, and I moved toward it, sidestepping stacks of books and newspapers, until I stepped into the kitchen to find Mrs. Bauer splayed on the laminate floor, a chair toppled beside her, her eyes alert and fixed on me. I gently helped her back up into a seated position, righted the chair, and then lifted her into it with some difficulty as she winced. She told me that she had woken early, and tried using the chair to fetch a tin of sardines from a top cupboard when the chair slid out from under her. She had then attempted to use the toppled chair to stand back up, only to slip again. I had left Mrs. Bauer lying alone on her kitchen floor for hours and I was furious with myself, and more unreasonably with Gabor for making me doubt my own senses, my intuition. I stammered a few empty words of solace to Mrs. Bauer, before offering to take her to the hospital, to which she batted her hand like she had at my nakedness so many years ago—"*Ich will nur meine verdammten Sardinen.*" I reached up and retrieved the tin, and then watched, impotently, as she went about toasting a piece of rye bread, buttering it, and placing three sardines on top.

"This is how you live to ninety," she said, holding up the piece of toast after taking her first bite. "Why are you hovering?"

"I think you should at least sit down."

"I've been on the floor all morning, I want to stand."

I knew there was no point in arguing with her. "Are you bruised? I'm worried you might have broken something."

"Oh, I'll probably have a bruise, I'm sure."

"Is there no one I can call? What about Lisbeth?"

"What is she going to do, I'm not on the floor anymore."

"I'm sure she would want to know that you had a tumble, no?"

My use of the German word *plumpsen* for "tumble" made Mrs. Bauer chuckle, which resolved into a cough, and a shake of her head, no, no she didn't want her daughter calling off work and driving in from Karow—to do what, fret over her? I felt a bit awkward watching Mrs. Bauer eat her breakfast, but I wasn't prepared to leave her on her own just yet, and I could see by the way she was standing that she was in more pain than she was letting on and would have trouble moving about after I left. Gradually, her pride relented, she sat down on a chair, and agreed that perhaps calling her daughter was the best course of action, and so we did. Lisbeth told her mother that she would drive straight over, and then Mrs. Bauer handed me the phone, and Lisbeth, whom I had seen regularly over the years though only ever in passing, thanked me and asked whether I might wait with her mother for the hour it would take for her to arrive, which of course I said I would. The prospect of an hour of Mrs. Bauer's company was rather daunting, if I was honest, given that we had never spent more than five minutes together in the thirty-some years of our acquaintance. I wrapped a fistful of ice cubes in a dish towel, and as Mrs. Bauer iced her thigh, we spoke of her daughter's family for some time.

"Is that her there?" I said, pointing to an old photograph atop a nearby hutch of Mrs. Bauer as a young mother, pushing a little girl on a sled.

"Yes, that's Lisbeth. That was on Teufelsberg."

"Teufelsberg?"

"Sometime in the late fifties, I suppose."

"Before the spy station."

"Yes, it was still a public park then, very good for sledding, and I always thought, well, why shouldn't I use it, I built the damn thing, after all," she said with another hoarse chuckle.

"Built it?" I asked, bemused, thinking for a moment that she meant the sled.

"No, the hill! My sister and I did."

For a moment it seemed as if she would say nothing more about it, but then she continued. She told me that she and her sister, Renate, had once lived in a cellar for three weeks in near-total darkness, they could touch each side with the tips of their fingers if fully extended, the walls blackened from coal storage. Three weeks of curses muttered to God, of prayers, of tins of preserves, of rainwater streaking in rivulets down into a metal bucket, enough for a few mouthfuls a day. The days of the firestorm were followed by the thunder of the Red Army passing overhead, and she and Renate had tried to make themselves as ugly as possible to the Soviets, hunching their backs, smearing their faces with coal dust, and wrapping themselves with burlap as "the Ivans" leered at them through the casement windows.

"They raped girls as young as eleven, sometimes groups of six, seven men," Mrs. Bauer said matter-of-factly, as she aligned the crumbs on her plate with her little finger. I marveled that we had been talking about sledding a mere two minutes earlier. She told me that one morning she and her sister heard voices speaking German in the street above, but still they waited another night and morning before finally sliding open the metal latch across the cellar door, emerging blinking and bent into the light, into the terrible silence of the dead, a smoldering wasteland, the charred husks of cars and buses, of bodies, churches gutted by fire, buildings shorn of their walls and leaving behind grids of multicolored rooms suspended in the air like phantom dollhouses. She looked around at the other haunted faces coming up from basements and sewers and realized that she now lived in a city of women.

"I just remember the dust. Everywhere. My throat was filled with this dust that was too thick to even swallow."

She watched a mother with her daughter picking through the rubble, gathering as much wood as they could carry home for fuel. She saw a family scavenging through a café, taking whatever they could—washbasins, torn curtains, pieces of a broken stove. She thought to herself: Is this how we are to live now? Like vultures, on the corpse of our own city?

"My sister and I were maybe fourteen or fifteen years old, and very—well—we had to be very careful, because the Americans were hardly much better than the Soviets."

I nodded, leaning against the counter in the fluorescence of Mrs. Bauer's kitchen. She then fell quiet again for a long moment, and I prompted with another question or two, after which she explained that she and her sister had moved in with a neighbor family, and began helping them dig out their home from the rubble. As a

Berliner of many years it was not new to me, how thousands of women had excavated their neighborhoods from the ruins, standing shoulder to shoulder, passing brick after brick between their chafed hands and out into the street. The bricks that could be reused were scrubbed of ash and stacked, and those that were shattered would be piled for disposal. Mrs. Bauer said she remembered thinking, at that rate, they would still be clearing Berlin a millennium from then, whole generations living and dying in the rubble, passing bricks between themselves until their hands bled, a Sisyphean fate, though he only had one rock to reckon with. The women worked without any plan. Sometimes debris would be thrown down a U-Bahn ventilation shaft and would have to be carted back out a couple of weeks later. At first they even worked without tools, though eventually tools were found, sledgehammers, pickaxes, hand winches, wheelbarrows, and soon the women set to dismantling buildings too damaged to rebuild, and breaking walls down into single bricks. As the summer wore on, the Allies issued a work order requiring all women of working age to assist with the cleanup, though only a few hundred really did, most seeing it as beneath them, this type of labor having once been the work of prisoners, and so mostly the work fell to private businesses, which were issued permits to hire women to do the clearing.

"Which is what happened with Renate and me, we took jobs with a construction firm, Karl Möbis Bauausführungen, to clear the city. We worked nine hours a day, with a twenty-minute break. At sixteen I had the hands of a builder," she said, smiling as if at a private joke.

Whatever could not be reused was thrown into the backs of lorries, eight hundred a day throughout the city, which ferried the loads out into the Grunewald, the ruins of Berlin dumped onto an ever-growing mound beside Teufelssee, until the mound grew over many years into a hill. And yes, for a few blessed years, before the Americans built their spy station atop it, the hill had been a public park, and in winter Mrs. Bauer would take her daughter sledding down its slope, the daughter who was now stuck in morning traffic on her way from Karow. Mrs. Bauer said she always found it strange that she might pass a woman in the street without remembering that they had once stood side by side in a long line ferrying out the remains of a collapsed building. When she was older, after Renate was gone, and the Americans had abandoned their station, and the hill had been returned to the public as an overgrown park, she would sometimes climb Teufelsberg, and she would sense her sister there, looking out over the glittering new city with her, trying to make sense of everything that had come to pass.

Though I did not know it at the time, that morning would be the last I would ever speak with Mrs. Bauer. Once Lisbeth arrived, and saw the bruising along her mother's calves, she would take her mother to the hospital, and at last put into motion the plans she had made to move her mother out from that ground-floor flat and into a nursing home a short drive from her, where Mrs. Bauer would never again have to replace a light bulb or ask her aging, bachelor tenant to do so for her.

By the first week of July, the photograph of the elderly nudist chasing Elsa through the meadow had become one of the summer's most popular memes on the Internet. With more boar sightings, more videos, and more visitors, the head of the forestry office was interviewed by the *Berliner Kurier*, and went on record confirming that the mother boar and her piglets would "regrettably have to be destroyed as a public safety priority." After the *Berliner Kurier* article, I started an online petition to save Elsa, and recruited Birgit and Gabor to help me circulate the link among their networks. Over several afternoons, I approached a number of longtime Teufelssee regulars in the meadow with the petition on my phone, asking them to sign it, all of whom did, including Vincenzo, Andrea, and Tommaso (I made note of their names as they did), who suggested we actually arrange a demonstration out front of the forestry office for later that week. I exchanged numbers with several other regulars I knew well but had never spoken to, including the dreadlocked and tutu-clad *soixante-huitard*, who I learned was named Evangeline, and the elderly couple with their cigars and striped umbrellas, who introduced themselves as Bruno and Anneliese, and I created a WhatsApp group to coordinate details for the protest.

"Why are you pouring yourself into this?" Birgit asked me, the evening before the demonstration, as we painted signs on my dining table. "Is it some kind of distraction?"

"You mean from the dead?"

Birgit held my gaze. "I'm worried about you."

"This is helping. You here, painting these signs with me. Besides, who will look out for Teufelssee if not us?"

"The forestry office. That's literally their responsibility."

"Well, I refuse to believe killing Elsa is good for Teufelssee, or the forest, or anyone, I think it's simply convenient, and they don't want a lawsuit on their hands if something happens, and I think that's a sick way for the world to be."

The B-side of the Au Pairs album that had been

playing came to an end, and the room slipped into silence as the turntable slowed to a stop and the stylus gently clicked back into its holder. We too fell quiet. I watched as Birgit cut out a photograph of Elsa she had printed on my laser-jet, ran a glue stick along its backside, and affixed it to the bottom corner of a sign.

"Why is it now, do you think, that they're appearing to you?" she asked at length.

"I don't know. I don't have an answer for that."

"And why you, and nobody else?"

"Well, who's to say nobody else? Perhaps men have been cruising the dead for years without ever realizing."

Birgit looked up and met my eyes. "Well, let me ask you this: What do you think they want with you? They must want something, Lukas, Sebastian, Thomas. Unless it's you who needs something from them."

I did not know whether Birgit was teasing me, or attempting to humor me, or even whether a part of her was inclined to believe me. I was not even sure whether I was inclined to believe myself; as far as I was concerned everything was in doubt, even my own perceptions. I mulled her question as I wiped my hands of paint with a wet paper towel. What was it that I needed? Surely nothing that they could provide me, whatever they were, flesh or figment, and frankly thank God I had a pig to focus my energies on, something to ground me to the world of the real, the world of action, of task and duty, lest I become as unmoored as Birgit and Gabor thought me to be.

The demonstration was held the following morning on the steps of the forestry office and drew nearly two dozen people, surpassing even my most ambitious expectations. Evangeline brought a megaphone into which she shouted, *"Finger weg von unserem Schwein!"* and trilled the bullhorn's siren with grating fervor; Birgit's ex-partner Antje, whom I had not seen in probably fifteen years, came with her wife, Jana, and their two children, Timo and Sasha, both of whom wore pig masks they had made of pink construction paper; Birgit and I distributed our homemade signs to those who wished to hold one; and Gabor drummed a steady beat on the stretched goatskin of his tabor, the one he had inherited from his great-uncle, a folk musician and martyr of '56, and which he always brought to marches, claiming every protest needed a heartbeat. Bemused forestry employees peered down at us from the second-floor windows, two local camera crews appeared, then the police, but though we were making a racket we were not barring anyone's entry to the building, and so the police stood by and let us have at it. As the protest neared the two-hour mark, the director of the forestry office emerged from the front doors of the building to jeers from the crowd. He held up his hands and announced that he had taken the public's concerns to heart, both the petition and the protest, and that Elsa and her offspring would be left in peace. Birgit embraced me with such force that I dropped my sign, and the crowd's jubilation drowned out the director's requests for everyone to kindly vacate the premises. The commuting of Elsa's death sentence was captured by both camera crews, and was broadcast that evening on the local news.

We celebrated our little David and Goliath victory with a round of drinks at a nearby bar, Gabor and I making variations of the same joke about being disease-harboring pigs ourselves and thus sharing a natural affinity. Birgit spent much of the evening talking with Antje, after Jana had taken Timo and Sasha home. After our third round, just as we were once more discussing Mrs. Bauer's story, and the questions I wished I'd had the presence of mind to ask, who should we see walking into the bar but the director of the forestry office and two of his colleagues. The director pretended not to notice us, but, realizing he had been spotted, turned and nodded in our direction, and after being handed his beer, he made his way over. As we shook hands, and I looked into his eyes, and I heard him speak in his reserved but earnest manner, I suddenly had an altogether different sense of him, not at all the stolid bureaucrat but a young Berliner who simply loved nature, loved the city's trees and animals, and had devoted his life to conserving them.

"I'm glad you all got your happy ending. But just so you're aware—two thousand wild boars are culled in this city every year as part of regular population control measures."

I was dumbstruck. "Two thousand?"

"Every year. In fact, it will probably be more this season, their numbers are exploding. They would completely destroy the ecosystem otherwise. But. You saved one," he said, raising his glass with a wry smile. "The famous one. I'm sure she's very grateful, for your sentimental intervention on her behalf."

Birgit asked what happened to all of the boars after they were culled; were they sent to butchers to use for meat? The director of the forestry office, after taking a sip of beer, informed us that the meat was inedible because the boars were radioactive. "From Chernobyl. And the nuclear bomb tests of the sixties."

I glanced at Gabor and Birgit. "The boars are radioactive because of Chernobyl?"

"A big part of their diet is underground fungi like deer truffles, which absorb radioactive cesium from the soil, which is partly why the boar population is exploding, because hunting and eating them is restricted."

I asked him how long the fungi in the Grunewald would be radioactive, and he said that, while no one knew for certain, the cesium-135 used in the nuclear weapons had a half-life of 2.3 million years.

As I walked Birgit home that evening, she tried to reassure me that knowing of the cull made our victory no less special, and Elsa's life no less worth saving, but I could not shake my embarrassment. I had thrown myself at a cause about which I knew essentially nothing. Elsa happened to be the specific radioactive boar I was fond of; had I really done all of this for myself, and why was it now that I needed to save a life so urgently?

"He never did tell us what they do with all of those boar bodies," I said as we reached Birgit's building. "Do you reckon they just have a giant bonfire?"

"I hate to say it, but I bet that would smell incredible."

Birgit invited me in for a nightcap, and as we sat at her kitchen table, nursing tumblers of the caraway-flavored Gilka Kaiser-Kümmel, her favorite digestif, which I had never developed a taste for, her gaze drifted to somewhere beyond my shoulder as she shook her head.

"Seeing Antje and Jana with the kids . . . I found it very hard."

"But you've seen them so many times."

"I know, but today—I don't know why, it really hit me differently. I think I finally have accepted that . . .

I'm alone." She smiled with an almost luminous sadness. "I'm lonely."

I put my hand on hers as she ran her tongue along her bottom lip. She brought her hand up to wipe her eyes and overturned the small sugar bowl on the table. "Shit," she muttered, trying to gather the spilled sugar into her hand before abandoning the effort, and then sitting in silence for a long while.

"We were never meant to be alone in the world."

"You're not."

She seemed to hold back, and I was suddenly embarrassed by my fast and feeble assurance, said more for my own comfort than hers.

"I remember—do you remember how I balked when I first heard Antje was getting married? And kids? I mean, how completely boring. I really couldn't imagine. I've spent my life talking about growing old with my friends, but I've been feeling . . . the limits of that. I'm not saying I regret anything. But. You and Gabor are not there with me at nights. Or in the mornings. And now there's only three of us. I feel like we're the last survivors clinging to the wreckage of a ship." She looked into her glass a moment, before taking a sip. "And what if one of us lets go, what then? Do the other two move in together? You laugh, but is it so crazy an idea?"

"Cohabitating with Gabor, can you imagine?"

She smiled at the thought, tracing her finger through the sugar, before looking back up at me. "It's harder to imagine being alone until the end. At the end."

Somewhere in the night came the two-tone cry of a police siren making its way through Zehlendorf, and then the pitch-bend as it passed Birgit's building, on its urgent way to another person's misfortune, some other crisis surely greater than ours that evening at the kitchen table. I gave her hand a small squeeze and told her that I would always be with her, and she broke into a throaty laugh. "I know you will, you bastard, and you'll haunt me just like Lukas and Sebastian when you're gone."

I did not, as per Gabor's suggestion, seek the counsel of a psychiatrist, and I would flatly lie whenever he asked me about it, something I had never done in our decades of friendship. Instead, I committed myself wholly to the task of solving the mystery of Teufelssee. I began keeping a logbook of my visits to the lake and the cruising grounds, making note of the men I encountered, the sex we had, the wildlife, the quality of light throughout the day. I was looking for patterns and anything that might fall outside of them. My logbook filled with entries, sometimes long, detailed paragraphs, other times short, cryptic jottings that would take me ages to decipher later if I even could. I knew well enough not to take photographs in the cruising grounds, though I was haunted by the regret of not having taken a single photo of Thomas during our final encounter, time-stamped evidence that would have put to rest the lingering question of chronology. If something strange, even mystical, was afoot, I realized I needed incontrovertible proof if I was to be believed, and if the thing that was amiss was my own mind, then documenting its decline would hold a value of its own, even if only to me. I spent every day that week at the lake, and hours after nightfall in the dark, wandering the pines, giving myself over to anyone who approached. It was less a hunger than a surrendering. It was on such nights that I felt closest to the dead, to a state of extreme porousness. In the darkness, I became a vessel for every man who had ever passed through these woods, letting their bodies possess mine and live once more through me. While joining myself with the bodies of strangers, our limbs, orifices, fluids becoming indistinguishable from one another's in the gleaming night, I wondered whether we might momentarily become one another, or new creatures altogether, immortal multi-limbed beings conjured by these arcane rites. Or what if it was pleasure that in fact lived through us, eternally shape-shifting and leaping between bodies so as to possesses us for a time, for all time, never to be extinguished?

On a humid Friday night, the air close and dense, after wiping myself clean with my balled-up underwear and buttoning up my jeans, I began making my way back toward where I had left my bike, unchained and trusting against a tall elm, when gradually I became aware of a pulse in the dark, through the forest, which seemed to emanate from the ground, like a heartbeat, low and reverberant, and as I walked through the shadows the throbbing grew louder, until I could feel it in my rib cage, and I followed it until I noticed a flickering light through the trees, which, when I emerged into the clearing, I realized was a bonfire, with silhouettes passing in front, a party, techno playing, people drinking, I could see tiny fireflies of cigarettes being lit, then my own heartbeat quickened with anger, adrenaline, and without giving a single thought to what I would say, I began striding across the sandy expanse toward the revelers—"Hey! Hey, you guys can't be doing this, you gotta put out this fire."

"Are you a cop?"

"No, I'm—"

"Then leave us the fuck alone."

"There's a fire ban—"

"Please, just fuck off."

"These are cruising grounds."

"You don't think we know that? We come here too."

"Everybody here is queer, man."

"Listen—"

"Just take a look around, every one of us is queer here."

"—if you keep having fires the police are going to start patrolling here—"

"It seems like you're the one being the cop here."

"—and if the cops start coming because of fires and parties, they will clamp down on everything."

"This is not just your forest, all right? All you old white faggots think this place is yours, but it's not."

"I'm not saying that—"

"'Cause that's what it sounds like, you're the one being the fucking cop."

I started kicking sand on the fire, and several of them grabbed me, both sides under the armpit, and pulled me away, shouting, and I tripped to the ground, winded, for a second I couldn't speak, until a young woman with cold hands and a pierced septum helped me up to my feet and brushed the sand off my back. I was trembling. She began to walk with me back across the clearing as I caught my breath, making sure I was okay, and perhaps ensuring that I wouldn't come charging back.

"Look, I get where you're coming from," the woman

said to me, "but you need to understand that for a lot of us here, like, we don't even feel welcome here during the daytime."

"Right, but we're in a drought—"

"Yeah, I know, but this is also about our safety at night. Having light, being together in a group, do you get that, it's not the same for us. We'll put out the fire, we'll clean up our bottles and trash, all of it, I promise you."

There was nothing more I could do or say; we all had to coexist in this forest on the borders of legality, and at times beyond them, and so I thanked this person, who was young enough to be my granddaughter, and I took her at her word that she would put out the fire, and bury the coals.

Following my late nights in the forest this summer, I began waking in the morning with a dull headache, just behind my eyes, which would throb more intensely whenever I coughed or bent over and for which painkillers offered little relief. I came to the formerly unthinkable decision to give up poppers, which I would bring even to the lake, and promised myself that, no matter where I roamed, I would be home in bed and asleep by midnight, and indeed both of these concessions made something of a difference, minimizing the frequency and intensity of my headaches, though they did not eliminate them entirely. Given the unrelenting heat, Gabor suggested I might be dehydrated, and insisted we were supposed to drink five liters of water a day, which I simply refused to believe, I mean how did our hunting-gathering predecessors even come by that much water throughout a given day, they would have had to crouch gulping streamside for hours. All the same, I began drinking more water, and all the same, the headaches continued.

"Is he okay with you showing me these?" I asked Gabor the following afternoon as I sat beside him in our usual spot by the lake, watching as he scrolled through photo after photo of a hirsute man lying supine in a sling, feet strung up in stirrups, and head zipped in a black leather hood.

"Oh, absolutely, he's already posted these. I mean—"

"Wow."

"Right?"

"How does he even do that?"

"With practice."

On one hand, I was astounded Gabor had taken home the director of the forestry office and fucked him the very night of our protest, but then, on the other hand, it was such a quintessentially Gabor thing to do that I didn't even feel the least bit indignant about it.

"He's cute, he's filthy, he's smart."

"How filthy are we talking?"

Gabor pulled up a Twitter account belonging to Eren, the director of the forestry office, and played a video of him tied to a Saint Andrew's Cross while being whipped by a cigar-smoking dom.

"This is his Twitter account? And he's a government employee?"

"Well, it's his anonymous account, you never see his face."

"But isn't he worried someone will recognize him, his tattoos? Couldn't he lose his job for this?"

"In the Berlin forestry department? Please."

I cocked my head to the side, as if a change of angle might help me see what Gabor found erotic about this video of his young lover being tortured. "I've never understood the masochism thing. Is it about daddy issues?"

"Honey, daddy issues? I mean, you could deconstruct this shit twelve ways to Sunday, all I know is sometimes it's just ecstatic to relinquish control like that, to feel something that intensely."

"So it's *jouissance*?"

"Oh, don't—" Gabor chortled and pointed his finger at me *j'accuse*. "Keep your fucking Lacan out of this, he's a piggy bottom who likes getting flogged, end of story, I'm seeing him again on Tuesday."

"Well, looks like an awful lot of effort to me."

"Says the man who spends his nights truffle-hunting dick in the forest. What good sex doesn't take effort?"

"Fair."

"Wait, is this the cruising diary you were telling me about?"

Gabor plucked the brown Moleskine from the front pocket of my knapsack and began flipping through its pages, squinting as he tried to read the various entries. "What's all this?" he asked, pointing to a hastily sketched map with annotations. *"Blue baseball cap, 7:13 p.m. fourth path near downed oak, northwest. Never returned."*

I paused. "I can't tell you."

"Why?"

"Because you're going to think I'm crazy."

"Oh, honey, that ship has long sailed."

I exhaled, and with considerable reservation began explaining to him that I had seen at least three, maybe four more men whose names I did not know, but whom I recognized from somewhere, somewhere in the distant past, perhaps decades ago, maybe I had been at a club with them once, or sucked them off in a bathroom stall, men who I noticed, usually at twilight, entering the forest and never returning.

"They go in. They don't come out. They don't leave."

Gabor stared at me for a long moment, his jaw set. "That's fucked up."

"I know."

"No, I mean you recording their comings and goings, that's fucked-up behavior."

"I'm not taking photographs or writing names—"

"I don't care—"

"It's just my diary—"

"I don't fucking care!"

My face flushed hot. Gabor had never shouted at me like that before.

"I just use one identifier like 'blue baseball cap,' or, or 'handlebar mustache'—"

"I don't care, it's creepy, I find it creepy and I don't like it. Besides, have you never considered these men simply left by a different route?"

"Every man retraces his steps, everyone leaves the way they came."

"You're insane."

I snatched the diary back. "I knew this is exactly what you'd say."

"Frankly, that's more disturbing than what I thought I was going to find."

"Mostly it's just a log of the sex I'm having."

"Wait, can I—"

Gabor reached over and took the diary back from me, opened it to the annotated map, and tore out the page in one firm, crisp gesture, before ripping it up and tossing the diary back to me. He then stuffed the confettied page into his pocket for later disposal. I felt as if I had just been slapped.

"Get your head checked, okay? I'm tired of this crap. Write about the dicks you take, I don't care, but stop watching when people come and go, and definitely stop jotting it down."

"I'm sorry, I—"

"Don't apologize to me, apologize to those men, except don't, please don't talk to them, just leave them alone."

I knew Gabor had said what he had said out of an abundance of concern, and I didn't even dispute his critique of my notebook, but it was how he had gone about it, the force, the violence of it, that was unforgivable to me; the tightly coiled rage from his childhood sprang forth like a ferocious jack-in-the-box once every few years, though thankfully, before that afternoon, never at me. Gabor was too prideful to admit that he had overreacted, and I felt too aggrieved to extend forgiveness, and so, at an impasse, we went a week without speaking, and then another. I felt abandoned by him, and to an extent by Birgit as well. I was alone in my confusion, and in my mounting urgency to find answers. As the summer neared its midway point, I was no closer to understanding what I had experienced, and though I had waited and watched, I had not yet reencountered Lukas or Sebastian or Thomas. I was clearly in need of more advanced methods than idle observation. I began making visits to the Freie Universität's rather utilitarian reading room, requesting from the stacks any books, diaries, or photographs I could find that pertained to Teufelssee, hoping to find some clue, some personal account or passing mention, of inexplicable occurrences that would shine new light on my own. To this end, I found nothing. Undeterred, I began taking the train out to Potsdam, to the Brandenburgisches Landeshauptarchiv, the region's main state archive. Formerly housed in Friedrich Wilhelm IV's stunning Orangery Palace in the Sanssouci gardens and modeled after the Villa Medici in Rome, the archive was regrettably moved in recent years to an utterly charmless white complex in the suburb of Golm, where it sat in what looked like a business park. I spent my afternoons seated in the same chair, at the same blond wood table in the carpeted quiet of the archive's main reading room. I happened upon several fascinating maps and geological surveys in advanced states of deterioration that I suspect had not been handled or studied in nearly two centuries, but after several days

I began to despair that again I would find nothing of real value to my search.

It was on what was to be my final visit that I happened upon a small tabloid article that set my heart racing. In a story from 2009, published in *Bild*, buried at the bottom right corner of page eight, I read about a young man found wandering naked and confused on the shores of Teufelssee. The man, who appeared to be in his late twenties, was spotted by two passing cyclists just after sunrise on July 6 of that year, shivering and disoriented, in the meadow that slopes upward from the shore. When the cyclists approached, offering assistance, the man claimed to be searching for his mother and sister, who had been sitting on a blanket in the crowded meadow only a few moments earlier, waiting for him as he swam. He insisted that he had been in the water for just a couple of minutes, had dived down, and upon surfacing discovered himself to be entirely alone. The cyclists were confused by this account, as it was dawn and there would be no sunbathers at the lake yet for several hours. The man then asserted that he was "not in his proper body," as the article phrased it, *nicht in seinem richtigen Körper*, a turn of phrase I found arresting. The cyclists waited with the man as police were called, and upon being questioned later at the station, the man claimed his name was Janis Pfeiffer, and believed the year to be 1989. The crux of the mystery, and my ensuing obsession with it, was revealed in the article's next sentence. Twenty years earlier, on July 5, 1989, a nine-year-old boy also named Janis Pfeiffer was reported to have disappeared while swimming at Teufelssee. The lake had been closed and dredged for two days following the disappearance, but a body was never found. It was thought at the time that Pfeiffer might have been abducted, and a missing persons file was opened under his name. That was the extent of the information contained in the newspaper article, two short paragraphs, made all the more captivating by its cryptic brevity. The questions I was left with upon finishing the article included: Did anyone question the man claiming to be Janis Pfeiffer about his childhood, and was he able to produce any irrefutable piece of evidence that he was, improbable as it might be, the same person? Was Janis Pfeiffer's family contacted, what was their reaction to this bizarre circumstance, and could they recognize or otherwise verify this man's identity? And if we were to believe this man's semi-mystical account of his experience, where did he "go," by which I mean vanish, between diving into the lake at the age of nine, and surfacing two decades later, and how was it that his body aged during this period, but he otherwise lacked any memory of this time lapse?

I photographed the article with my phone, and when I showed it to Birgit that evening at her flat over dinner, she tutted, "Poor kid. Probably some strung-out queen who got mugged while cruising. Sounds familiar," she added with a chuckle, but I wasn't in the mood to laugh.

"But why invent such an elaborate story?"

Birgit sighed, summoned patience, and replied, "I don't know. Maybe he had some kind of psychotic break." She began to theorize that perhaps the man had gone to the lake the previous day, swimming and sunbathing nude, before suffering some kind of mental health episode, and had spent the night alone in a state of bewildered agitation.

"Maybe the story of Pfeiffer and the lake resided somewhere in the back of his mind, and for whatever reason he adopted it in his psychosis."

But what of the extraordinary alignment of dates? I asked. To this Birgit had no response. I could tell it pained her to talk about anything related to my "obsession," as she now called it. The short article and the mysterious circumstances it described preoccupied my thoughts over the proceeding days, but as much as I searched online for further information, I found nothing, not even the *Bild* article had been digitized. Birgit encouraged me to just let it go, it was not worth fixating on. *Bild* was a trashy tabloid, and the article was most likely fanciful conjecture, a staff writer's imagination given free rein. And yet, there was something about it that stood apart from the usual tabloid horrors and mysteries, not just because it involved Teufelssee but also because I found something lyrical in its quiet longing and enigma, a boy diving into a lake in the dying days of the Cold War and surfacing decades later into the solitary night of adulthood, into a world remade. The story did not seem to have caught anyone's attention, I found no mention of it on any blog or social media, and I began to wonder if I was the only person alive who was even aware of it. Against my initial better judgment, I decided to message every Janis Pfeiffer I could find on social media who was roughly the appropriate age and residing in Germany, of which there were seven. Of these seven, only one wrote back, with a terse *Verpiss dich*. It was after this that I finally began to give some credence to Birgit and Gabor's concern that I may be in the midst of some kind of manic episode.

As the drought intensified, I gradually became aware of a presence as I lay at night in the permeable state just before sleep. Teufelssee, somehow both dark and luminous, was aware of me. The lake could perceive me, prone in my bed, and it knew fully my heart, and my longings, and that I sought something unnameable from it. It was a quiet terror, like a slumbering god suddenly opening the terrible whites of its eyes in the pitch black. As I lay there, being perceived by Teufelssee, the lake began to reveal its secret to me, but it was more than I could comprehend, more than any one soul could bear, beyond the limits of my body, and in that moment I woke with a start, my sheets damp with sweat. As much as I could grasp, I understood that there was a force that dwelled within Teufelssee so vast, so heavy and ancient, it bent the very fabric of reality around it, bent desires, lives, and lured us to our destruction, to the very making and unmaking of meaning. I rose from my bed, slipped my bare feet into my tired trainers, and began to walk through the chilled night toward the Grunewald, and soon entered the enveloping blue of the forest, this time with intention—I was going to find Lukas, or Thomas, or Sebastian, or whoever else lay in wait for me, I would walk deep into the darkness, as deep as it took, and I would present myself to Teufelssee, and I would demand from the shadows that they appear. At that hour, the woods were a simmering madness, everywhere movement, terrible and invisible, I felt unseen eyes upon me, I felt myself being trailed, the rustle of footsteps behind me, but each time looking back I saw no one. The sound of my own quickening breath was deafening. I felt myself becoming an unspooling clew, losing more and more of myself with every step through the maze. What would be left of me by dawn? Upon arriving at the lake, I found it the color of quicksilver, a great metal sheet reflecting moonlight, and, as I stopped on its shores, a sound escaped me, my own voice terrifying, I had no control over it. I screamed the language of the dead, and yet nothing appeared, and my voice, after echoing four times over the water and back, diminished into oblivion. I did not encounter a single being, living or otherwise, not by the lake, nor as I stalked through the pine glades of the cruising grounds.

By the time I returned to my flat that morning, the dull ache behind my eyes had returned, and over the next four days progressed into a full migraine. Birgit began making daily visits to check on me, and as I sat across from her at my kitchen table, eating the soup she had brought, she shared her concern that I was experiencing some kind of psychosis.

"Or perhaps now just at the end of it."

"It's a migraine."

"It's not just the migraine. You haven't been yourself. You're distracted, even at dinner, it's like you're not in the room. Where do you go? Are you wandering the forest, looking for ghosts? Since Thomas passed, it's just been—"

"This is not about Thomas."

She sighed, and hesitated a moment. "I don't know if this is helpful, or if you want to hear this, but I was reading about delayed-onset PTSD."

"Birgit."

"Latent responses to trauma, grief, that can manifest in the most strange and unexpected ways sometimes years after the fact, and I don't mean Thomas. Maybe he was a trigger, I don't know, but I mean the ones you buried deep, in the past, Lukas, Ingo, Andreas, Mathias, Sebastian, all of them, you've been talking about them all summer, every conversation, when I haven't heard you mention their names in years. Decades."

"That's not true—"

"It is. You buried it, all of it. But I was there, all right, with you, with Lukas, after he left the hospital, emptying his bedpan, cleaning his sheets—"

"You don't think I remember?"

"This is maybe the first time I've heard you speak his name in thirty years."

I fell quiet. I then thanked Birgit for the food, and told her I needed to rest, which she rightly took as her cue to go. She urged me to seek out an assessment, and I told her that even if I were losing my mind, I had no desire to sit with a stranger talking about my long-dead lovers, and she threw up her hands and called me incurably British. She conceded that there was no way she could force me into therapy, but she was worried enough to arrange and accompany me to a doctor's appointment the following week, after which a referral was made to a neurologist. When I wasn't running errands, or replying to neglected correspondence, I was often lying in bed with the curtains drawn and a cold compress folded over my eyes. As I lay there, Birgit's words would play on my mind. Was all of this some elaborate, latent PTSD response? God, the very thought exasperated me, I was so tired of that kind of therapizing lens being placed over every facet of our lives and sexual identities, it felt so flattening and false and disempowering, and yet I couldn't discount the possibility that there was some truth to it. Nor could I shake thoughts of Lukas.

Lukas did not know how long he had been living with HIV, but was diagnosed with AIDS in 1993, and that November I took him on a trip to the Adriatic. He had been to very few places outside of Berlin, and it was his wish to see as much of the world as possible while he could. We rode the Belgrade-bound train from the Montenegrin coast, along cliff edges and through tunnels blasted into mountain rock by thousands of young communists under Tito, sharing our compartment with two Orthodox priests who surreptitiously smoked in the rattling corridor, and as the train climbed higher, we decamped to the dining car, where we drank Arabic coffee with the grounds left in, thick as crude oil, the heat of the coffee softening the plastic disposable cups in our hands. We watched the snow blow out from the sides of the train like wings as we crossed over the highest trestle on the continent, soaring above the turquoise ribbon of the Mala Rijeka, below us a winterscape of medieval villages dotting a valley like a Bruegel painting, and as we did, Lukas muttered to himself that even if humans lived another million years, they would never create anything so beautiful as Europe. I thought of all the old regimes, old empires, old faiths layered on top of one another like geological strata as we passed through forests that, within a matter of months, would echo with gunfire, before we plunged through another tunnel, and in the darkness I found my own face suddenly staring back at itself in the window. From Belgrade we journeyed northward, to Istria, and took the ferry from Trieste to Venice. We spoke of dead friends while drinking grappa in the lounge, before huddled couples began assembling on the front deck to watch the campaniles slowly emerge from the soupy gray twilight, wisps of murmured wonder escaping our lips in the cool air as the lagoon came into focus, moving at once forward through light and backward through time, a shiver running through me and not from the cold, to be alive, my God, to be alive and beside this man I still loved.

St. Mark's Square was flooded by the *acqua alta,* and the doorman of our hotel said a dolphin had been spotted that morning in the Grand Canal. Later, as we walked through Verona, a wayward flock of sheep clattered into the Piazza delle Erbe, overturning café tables and smashing small cups of espresso and bottles of Fanta against the paving stones. I turned to see Lukas smiling at the mayhem from behind his sunglasses. Friendship with Lukas never felt like a consolation but an ever-renewing intimacy, and we rediscovered it afresh each day as we woke up beside one another. Sometimes we would hold each other for an hour or so before rising, nestled together, as the morning light brushed over us. I had long since learned the language of Lukas's body. Over the years there had been many casual speakers, but I alone was fluent. He also grated my nerves like no other. He became loud when he drank, and while intensely bright was oddly incurious about history, his eyes glazing over if I spoke for longer than three sentences about a topic he didn't have some prior knowledge of, and he had an insouciant way of paying for absolutely nothing, and it wasn't so much that he was cheap or poor, for he loved spending lavishly on his own clothes, but he was chronically ungenerous, and accustomed to accepting gifts, particularly from older men. Everything about Lukas felt present tense, he had always lived as if no distant future existed, at least not for him, and this was how I loved him, as a deeply burning present. It was too painful to allow ourselves the fantasy of future projection, to imagine what it might have been like to grow old together, because we both knew, without having to say it, that we had been robbed.

We stayed for a week in the town of Lusevera, nestled in the foothills of Monte Tanarobo, where we befriended the elderly neighbor of the family who had rented us their home. The woman, who spoke Friulian first and Italian sparingly, was old enough to have had a mother who knew a Friuli independent of Italy, and she spoke of a postwar moment when the region was filled with the restive desire for independence, an independence that Pier Paolo Pasolini so desired that he founded a pro-devolution party, Movimento Popolare Friulano. She told us of how members of her family, centuries ago, had been *benandanti*, men and women who left their bodies as they slept to wander, in spirit form, through the fields and forests beyond their village to battle witches who threatened their harvest. The *benandanti* were all born with cauls on their heads, which marked them as having the special ability to take part in these visionary excursions. On select nights between the Ember Days, the spirits of the male *benandanti* would leave their sleeping bodies and venture into battle with the *malananti*, armed only with sorghum stalks, while the spirits of the female *benandanti* would travel to a great feast, where they danced in processions with animals and other spirits, and learned who in their village would die in the coming year. These were the traditions of the peasant fertility cult with ancient roots in the foothills, which were later cast as the machinations of the devil by local priests during the Inquisition.

The final week of July, I held the leash of Lisbeth's disagreeable terrier as Lisbeth and her husband removed about a dozen cardboard boxes of Mrs. Bauer's possessions. All the rest would be disposed of, Lisbeth informed me, gesturing toward the half-emptied flat, decades of furniture, books, newspapers, CDs, clothes, and all other manner of accumulated life to be dispersed through the city, into charity shops and dumpsters, and ultimately folded back under the earth. As I returned the leash to Lisbeth's hands, she assured me that she and her husband had no plans for the house for the time being, and would find a new tenant for the ground floor before the summer was through. I then shared with Lisbeth the remarkable conversation I had had with her mother, and marveled at how close I had come to having never heard her story about

Teufelsberg, despite my living just a floor above her for thirty-some years.

A knowing smile passed across Lisbeth's face. "Yes, quite a story, isn't it?" she replied, rather ambiguously.

"Why do you say it like that?" I asked.

I could see Lisbeth consider her words. "I think my mother—I think it's possible when you live through what she did, it—it can warp the stories we tell about ourselves. And sometimes we fill in the blanks, or take stories as our own that never even happened to us."

"You don't believe her?"

"I don't know, to be honest. I think some of it is certainly true. But I also know there are inconsistencies. Was she really a Trümmerfrau? That seems unlikely to me. And she talks about her sister, Renate, walking in the forest with her while pushing me in a stroller, or watching us sledding, but her sister died during the war. Just things like that."

I fell quiet, my mind flitting back over the details of my conversation with Mrs. Bauer while Lisbeth locked the door to the flat, and after a somewhat awkward will-we-won't-we hug goodbye, I waved her and her husband off in their car. As the car disappeared from view down the street I felt my headache return, and by the time I made it back upstairs it was all I could do to crawl into bed, where I stayed until evening. I had begun to wonder whether the headaches were caused by my ever-waning eyesight, the result of a lifetime spent reading in tents by headlamp, the fine print of ordnance maps in dim archive rooms, and dense tomes on long-haul flights by overhead cabin light. I made an appointment with an optometrist, but she assured me that there was nothing wrong with my eyes. By the time I had my appointment with the neurologist, the one arranged thanks to Birgit's intervention, I had almost forgotten it had been scheduled. After a preliminary consultation, the neurologist scheduled an expedited MRI for the following week. Two days after my MRI, I was called by the radiologist, and told the scans showed a tumor in my parietal lobe. Gabor accompanied me to a follow-up appointment, where tests revealed the tumor to be a glioblastoma, both malignant and aggressive. The oncologist explained that treatment would involve surgery followed by concurrent radiation and chemotherapy, and emphasized that this would offer me a few additional months, not a cure.

At long last it seemed the death I always felt I had cheated in my thirties had found me. My first thought was that there was so much reading I had yet to finish. Perhaps at last I should start *Don Quixote*. The second was that I did not want to spend what little time I might have left in hospitals. I would rather take four months at the lake than twelve in a cancer ward. I wanted to lay my body atop the warm grass and watch the sky shift above me, I did not want my last experiences of Earth to be the waiting rooms and corridors of the Charité Comprehensive Cancer Center, shuffling around an IV pole in a backless gown, chemotherapy chemicals and imaging dyes pumping through my veins. My decision felt self-evident to me, even my oncologist was sympathetic, though it upset Birgit and Gabor deeply, as if it were a personal affront to them. They claimed my judgment was impaired, that I was still in the throes of my so-called mania, Birgit going so far as to theorize my forgoing treatment was actually a perverse manifestation of my lifelong fear of death. She and I argued ferociously about it for about a week, I thought we were going to come to blows at one point in the produce aisle of a Spar, and then the argument transformed into a mostly one-sided exchange of videos and voice notes over WhatsApp. No matter how much I insisted or explained, I could not persuade either of them to come around to my reasoning, and so I stopped trying. Still, the news of my illness had gone a long way toward cauterizing the wound in my friendship with Gabor. He seemed almost relieved to have something on which he could now squarely pin my hallucinations, as he called them, and to focus his caregiving energies.

My desire to see out the rest of my days at Teufelssee found itself in conflict with a heavy depression that set in following my diagnosis. I locked myself in my flat for several days, and began to notice small moths whenever I opened the cupboard doors in my kitchen, particularly the pantry, where I discovered they had laid eggs in an opened box of oatmeal. Once, while heating coffee on the stovetop, one fluttered past my face, and I began to clap my hands and chase after it through the kitchen, and as it continually evaded me, its will to live filled me with a kind of strange élan, and I conceded that its desire for life was stronger than my desire to end it. I never again attempted to kill any of them, and resigned myself to an uneasy coexistence. I began to sleep more during the days, which was highly unlike me, I don't know whether because my body demanded it or my depression did, but invariably I found myself dreaming more of Lukas, dreams both vivid and long, of us traveling together over many days and weeks in distant countries, only to wake disoriented on my sofa in the diminishing evening light. Often, we were on some version of our last trip together.

After our time in Italy, Lukas and I had made a second trip the following spring through the Benelux, during which we bickered nonstop like an old married couple. Lukas was just getting over a bout of shingles, and everything I did seemed to annoy him. Whenever he grew sharp with me, I became sullen and quiet, which only inflamed his irritation. The weather didn't help matters, being misty, gray, and unseasonably cool, even for April. While in Bruges, we connected with a friend and former colleague of mine, Maes, who gave us a personal tour of the municipal archives where he now worked, and among the stories he told us was one that utterly fascinated Lukas about how the silting-up of the Zwin in the early sixteenth century led to an increase of public burnings of sodomites. As Maes explained it, in 1134, a great storm broke through the Flemish coast and carved a fifteen-kilometer tidal inlet that, through another channel, suddenly offered sea access to the formerly inland city of Bruges, and caused the city to rise in prominence as one of the foremost centers of European trade. But this new waterway and economic lifeline, named the Zwin, began to fill with silt from the late thirteenth century onward, and by 1500 it had grown so shallow as to render it unusable, cutting off Bruges again from the sea. As merchants shifted their business activities to nearby Antwerp, Bruges stagnated, and it was during this time of economic decline and hardship, when scapegoats were sorely needed, that an explosion of sodomy cases were brought forward and prosecuted by municipal authorities. In the public records, Maes had found a marked increase in sodomy trials, convictions, and public burnings in the Grote Markt between the years

1450 and 1525. From 1509 onward, the burnings were presided over by the local dogcatcher Wissel Geerts van Utrecht, who was purportedly a friendly man who tried to cheer the sodomites up with jokes or songs before setting the bundles of straw at their feet alight. I was astounded by the focus with which Lukas listened to Maes, it was so out of character, and I felt strangely jealous, to the point of quiet petulance, when he had shown only the most fleeting patience or interest in any of the historical accounts I had shared. Lukas was so transfixed by Maes's story, in fact, that on parting ways outside the archives, he turned to me and stated that he wished to write a book about the burnings. I smiled at first, thinking he was joking, but Lukas continued to talk about this prospective book with utter seriousness over lunch, and repeatedly for the rest of the trip, of the research he wished to undertake, and his plans to return to Bruges in order to write it, to which I simply nodded and remained silent. It was plainly evident, surely even to Lukas, that he would never return here and never write this book, and naturally this became another matter over which we fought, after he exploded at me for my lack of faith in his capacity. In the hotel stairwell, and all down the length of the corridor to our room, he shouted that I was "emotionally retarded" and insufferably pretentious and long-winded, like traveling with a guidebook he couldn't turn off. This nadir of the trip coincided with the worst days of rain, which beat down all the white petals from the flowering trees onto the asphalt. One afternoon we left our hotel room only once to fetch pastries and coffee from the nearby café, and otherwise napped and read in bed, exchanging hardly more than a dozen words between us. In my notebook from that week I wrote only the words: *how a single storm so transformed a landscape, that, through a chain of causality, contributed to the burning of sodomites in a market square centuries later.* Then, several days later, as Lukas and I were killing time in Antwerp before our train, we came upon a small convent garden filled with parrot tulips, and as church bells began to toll in the distance, the sun suddenly broke through the clouds, and I felt its warmth on my arms and my face for the first time all year, and inexplicably my eyes filled with tears, and I turned to Lukas, who smiled with confusion at me, but extended his arms all the same, taking me into them, and we hugged one another fiercely and with a love that exceeded any I had ever known.

After my diagnosis, I let Gabor's and Birgit's calls go unreturned for several days, until at last they persuaded me to join them at the lake. When we arrived we found the meadow more crowded than it had been all summer, even during the height of Elsa's fame. We decided to walk into the forest, to the clearing, where we set up our blanket in a patch of morning shade. After an hour we were met by Eren, who had quite quickly become something of a fixture in Gabor's life. Eren joined us in our toplessness, pulling off his shirt to reveal a thick, dark coat of body hair that put even Gabor's to shame, extending up his neck and merging unbroken with his beard, and resolving into great swirls over each of his pectorals. If there was any professional conflict with the director of the forestry office sitting half naked in a known cruising spot in the Grunewald, it troubled him little. He had brought a thermos of coffee and *katmer*, a type of sweet *börek* covered in a sprinkling of crushed pistachios, which we all enjoyed while talking about everything we could think of except for my illness. For a time we sat listening to the forest, the wind washing through the nearby boughs, birdsong, the hum of insects, distant conversations and laughter from other groups, and, closing my eyes against the sun, I watched phosphenes dance across my lids. Birgit lay back, resting her head on my thigh, looking up at the light through the canopy, while Gabor and Eren conversed quietly between themselves, just across the blanket but a world away, as I leaned back, my hands in the warm earth through which I could feel thin roots on my fingertips. As our patch of shade extended and eventually claimed the entirety of the clearing, Gabor and Eren rose, and announced they were going to take a stroll down the paths. By now Birgit was fast asleep on me, and I smiled and nodded farewell to the lovers. For a while, I watched the comings and goings in the clearing, before looking down and noticing the flutter of Birgit's eyelids. It was a calm and patient way to be, attached like that to another person, connected by means no less intimate than sex, by the deepest bonds of love, the moment as fragile as the surface of a bubble. I found myself nearly holding my breath so as not to rouse her. How wars could be fought over sacred land and holy sites was something that I had had the privilege to understand only intellectually, but for a fleeting moment, as I sat there, I understood it on some deeper, visceral level. If I had anything resembling a faith, it was this, this face on my thigh, my hands in the still-warm forest sand in the lengthening shadow of evening, I believed in this.

Just then, in the distance, came a great blast, followed by several more in quick succession, and Birgit jolted awake, blinking and wiping her face in confusion, as we both turned toward the north, where the booming seemed to originate.

"What the hell was that?"

It sounded as if the city were under aerial attack. Men began reemerging from the underbrush into the clearing, unsettled by the explosions that continued every five to ten seconds, and conferring with one another about what could possibly be happening. Birgit and I stood as we saw Gabor and Eren approaching at a pace down a nearby path. "Are we at war, then?" Gabor asked wryly, wiping sweat from his face, and downing the contents of a water bottle as Eren pulled on a shirt. We agreed to pack up our things and try to find a higher vantage point. There was always the possibility of terror, I thought, as we walked briskly through the pines, if this last quarter century had taught us anything it was that terror was a fact of the modern city, but terror from where, a far-right insurgency, an Islamist retaliation, a preemptive strike from a hostile state, or some nascent horror we had not yet even imagined? As the rumbling blasts continued, we made our way toward the lake, though eventually took a right along the main path, and started up the slope of Teufelsberg, climbing its worn footpaths toward the great white ruined domes of the former listening station, at which point I began to smell smoke, and upon nearing the top of the hill I saw extending over the northern reaches of the Grunewald a billowing gray plume. A crowd of onlookers was assembling on the hilltop, there were nearly forty by the time we arrived, and more ascending behind us, some scaling the exterior of the abandoned station to get a better view. "What's been hit?" I asked. Birgit was failing to find any news story about it yet on her phone, and brought up Google Maps in an effort to discern what was burning. When I looked over at Eren, his phone was to his ear, and he was mid-conversation with a colleague. "It's the munitions dump," he said to us, keeping his voice low. "All the confiscated fireworks get dumped there, unused ammunition, even old World War II bombs whenever they're found."

"Jesus Christ," Gabor murmured. "Some kind of fire must have broken out."

"Maybe from the heat," Birgit mused.

"Why the hell would they put a giant powder keg in the middle of the Grunewald?" Gabor asked.

"Well. Where else would you suggest they put it?"

The three of us stood there, by turns distressed and transfixed, watching the smoke extend through the northern reaches of the parkland as Eren finished his call.

"I need to go," he said as he pocketed his phone.

"Of course."

"Do you think it will reach the lake?" Birgit asked.

"Absolutely not." And with that Eren kissed Gabor, and hugged Birgit and me goodbye, before setting off down the hill at a run.

Birgit remained troubled. "Do you think people down there even realize? On the shore?"

The three of us began our descent, not running, for

there was no immediate danger, but swift enough to leave us winded by the time we reached the bottom. As we arrived in the crowded meadow, I noted that there was, in fact, no view of the gray plume, nor could one smell smoke or even hear the rumble of the explosions over the general din. The three of us dispersed through the crowd and began approaching people with the photos of the smoke cloud we had taken on our phones, describing the situation, and the distance, and while some people seemed confused or irritated by our interruption, others appeared grateful and, in the case of two families, began to pack up their things, whistling their kids in from the water and helping them into their clothes and shoes. Vincenzo, Andrea, and Tommaso had not yet arrived that morning, but Evangeline was there, as were Bruno and Anneliese, and I shared with them what I knew. They chuckled when I mentioned the munitions plant, and then shrugged as if to say: *It's always something, isn't it?*

The blaze ultimately spread through fifteen thousand square meters of bone-dry forest in a matter of hours, reaching temperatures in excess of seven hundred degrees Celsius. The extraordinary heat, and the fear that two unexploded Second World War bombs would detonate, kept fire crews at bay, forcing them to use water cannons and drones. Boars from the forest began appearing on the streets south of Schlachtensee, scampering through intersections and traipsing across the lawn of the Haus am Waldsee. A sow and her boarlet were hit and killed by a car on Argentinische Allee while trying to cross to the grass median. The military set up a thousand-meter perimeter zone around the fire, closing train lines, barricading the nearby highway, and began cutting a five-kilometer firebreak through the forest. The smoke plume was still visible from my flat that night as I went to bed, underlit by the glow of the city and pulled over us like a great blanket as we slept.

I visited Lukas twice a week in the final months of his life when he lived with Birgit, hardly as much as I should have, or as much as I had wanted to, out of cowardice, surely, but also denial. I managed to convince myself that we had more time together, as if taking for granted the time we did have would somehow extend it. I honored trivial social commitments, dinners, opening nights, as if by insisting on the normal continuation of my life I could insist on the same for his. I never knew quite what to say during those last visits, when everything that came out of my mouth sounded so unbearably glib, any expression of affection both insufficient and inappropriate. In the weeks before Lukas died, I could see death staring back at me from his eyes, with such intensity I struggled to hold his gaze for any length of time, which he surely noticed, being such a difference from the days when I would pour myself as deeply as I could into them, our faces a foot apart in bed, in our tent, in a lake. When I looked at my own reflection, I saw the sickness already in myself, his sunken sockets, his pallor. I scoured my body daily for signs. I knew it was likely only a matter of time until the wasting of his musculature, the protrusion of his rib cage, the plum-colored lesions on his chest and buttocks would be mine. Sickness terrified me, because death terrified me, and I sometimes wondered whether I became an archaeologist as a way of besting death, as a way of retrieving remnants of life from the dusty desiccated grip of un-being. To unearth remains was to reclaim something of life from the oblivion of unknowing, and I wanted the same for myself, should any part of me persist into the distant future, to be held and considered in that way. When Birgit called me, distraught, to tell me that she had returned home from a brief errand to find Lukas had died, I am ashamed to admit that I felt a release, a weight lifting from my chest as if it were the burden of my own soul finally escaping my body, and I walked around in that strange lightness for almost two hours until nightfall, when it all crashed down upon me in the shower, and I sobbed until the water ran cold.

It took local brigades three days to fully extinguish the munitions depot fire. The blaze did not come within a kilometer's reach of the lake, nor the cruising grounds, but something had shifted perceptibly within the Grunewald in the days thereafter, not just in the visitors, but, it seemed, in the very air and ground itself, as if the forest were lying in wait for the next calamity. The first Saturday after the fire, Gabor, Eren, and I returned to the sand-swept clearing, Birgit having taken the day to write at home, working on a long-delayed article on Hohle Fels that she had promised to *Archaeology* magazine. Eren was exhausted, having worked nonstop since the previous Saturday, liaising between different fire departments, the city, and the military in deciding which paths should be reopened, which areas required immediate remediation, and what would have to wait for the following spring. He recounted for us with mounting frustration the various communication breakdowns, how his office was being used as the catchall cleanup service, despite having its funding cut to the bone, and how generally ill-prepared the city was for such a disaster. As Eren spoke, and I held my hand to my brow against the midday sun, I noticed three police officers strolling across the clearing toward an elderly man with a large, hard belly being fellated by a leaner, sinewy man of similar age on a blanket. Gabor saw the look on my face and turned, his mouth falling open in shock. In all our years cruising at Teufelssee we had never seen police in the clearing, they knew well enough not to walk down our paths, lest they have a public relations crisis on their hands. For these officers to saunter into the heart of the cruising grounds was not just a breach of long-standing convention, it was a declaration of war.

"You just know they've been waiting for any half excuse to come in here and fuck with us," Gabor said. "And now they have the fire ban to enforce."

From where we sat, we could not hear the exchange between the officers and the elderly men, but it appeared to be escalating into an argument. Gabor and I rose from our blanket, and, followed with some reluctance by Eren, began walking toward the confrontation, as did several others in the clearing. As we neared, I overheard what was unfolding in German.

"And minding our business is a 'public nuisance,' now, is it?"

"Sir, this is a public forest, you are in full view here, and there has been a complaint."

"Who complained? That's bullshit."

"You're in broad daylight, I could see you from fifty meters away on that path."

"Oh, you were looking that hard, were you?"

"We have families and kids in these woods."

"Not on these paths."

"On the path I was, yes, there are. You guys have been getting more brazen lately, and—"

"You guys?"

"—and there have been complaints."

"Oh, so there's been multiple complaints, now?"

"Yes, and we are obliged to follow up on them."

Murmurs of discontent rose from around the clearing as one of the officers began drawing up fines for both men, and upon being handed his ticket, the man with the beach-ball belly tore it up with defiant flourish.

"*Verdammter Bullerei!*" a man in his thirties shouted at the officers from the other side of the grove, which encouraged others.

"*Bullenschweine!*"

"*Geh und fick dich selbst!*"

Gabor joined the chorus of dissent, unleashing a torrent of vitriol at the officers from what sounded like the deepest recesses of his soul, a reservoir of resentment, of loathing filled not just by his years in Germany, but by Viktor Orbán, and all the kleptocrats and thugs of

Fidesz, and earlier tyrannies still, perhaps right back to the schoolyards of Székesfehérvár. "*Verdammte Faschisten!*" Gabor's voice cut above all others, and his sheer size drew all attention toward him. "*Aussteigen*," he yelled, pointing in the direction of the path the officers had used to enter the clearing. "*Aussteigen!*" By now, at least five men were filming on their phones. One of the officers started shouting back at Gabor, telling him to calm himself, they had the right to patrol the forest, but Gabor only raised his voice further, accusing them of targeting and intimidating us, and the officers warned Gabor, threatening him with arrest if he continued, which of course only inflamed him further, he called them fascists, AfD pigs, "Gabby, please," Eren implored, grabbing his lover's arm, all the while I was at a loss for words, everything happening faster than I could process, "Arrest me for fucking what?" Gabor was shouting. "For sitting here in this forest, you're going to come in here and fucking arrest me?" And then he took a step forward, inches from the officer's face, and I knew that was it, the officer grabbed Gabor's right arm, and brought it around his back, while another grabbed his left arm and began to submit him to the ground with considerable difficulty, as the third officer fumbled with a pair of handcuffs, the entire clearing erupting, dozens of men shouting, pushing in, phones in their hands. As Gabor was being cuffed, he fell strangely quiet, though there was now such a clamor that perhaps he felt nothing more needed to be said. He wore a look of satisfaction on his face, as if claiming some kind of victory. Once he was cuffed, the officers began leading him out of the clearing, and Eren and I walked alongside the sorry procession, peppering the officers with questions. "*Wohin bringst du ihn?*" To which we were met with stone-faced silence. For a moment, I stepped back and took in the utter surreality of the scene, of Gabor being led out of the grove in his fetters. Their pound of flesh. They had made their example of him, as they had perhaps been subconsciously seeking to do all along, just as he had sensed, and, by helping them do so, he got them to prove his point. He was never one to lose an argument, no matter the cost.

Gabor was brought to the Polizeidirektion 2-Abschnitt 26 on Rudolstädter Straße for processing, charged with the verbal assault and intimidation of three police officers, and told that he would receive a notice in the mail informing him of his court date. Birgit, Eren, and I waited in the lobby of the station for him to be discharged. He was in a practically exuberant mood when he finally was, making wisecracks about the entire process. Birgit summoned an Uber on her phone, and while we waited for our car, Gabor joked that he would proudly frame whatever court summons he was served.

"I'm glad you can both laugh about it," Eren said, glancing at me coolly, as I chuckled.

"Oh please," Gabor replied.

"Maybe, as a Muslim, the police are not so funny to me."

"You're as Muslim as I am."

"Really? In their eyes, you think that?"

"I'm just saying—"

"When you laid into those officers, did my safety, my job, did anything other than yourself cross your mind, or were you—"

"Oh, I'm sorry for not thinking of your career just then."

Eren shook his head, in a quiet rage. "You want some kind of award, an Oscar maybe, for your little performance? For standing up to some fascists, as you called them, sure, maybe they were, maybe they jerk off to photos of Alice Weidel—"

"Eren, I was literally chased out of Hungary for writing and organizing against Fidesz, I'm not—"

"Yes, and you're celebrated for it! You have tenure for it! And what about my parents? My sisters, my uncles and aunts, where are their accolades?"

"What are you even talking about?"

For a moment, it was as if Eren did not even know where to start. He then began to recount how, earlier that week, on the street where he grew up in Neukölln, where his elderly parents still lived, neighbors woke to find white swastikas graffitied across the front doors of four apartment buildings occupied predominantly by Turks, Kurds, and Syrians.

"Thankfully not my parents' building, but one of them was where my father's sister and her family live. And the parents of childhood friends of mine."

"That's terrible, but all the more reason—I mean, why not celebrate someone standing up to these motherfuckers, then?"

"Because every single day my parents, my cousins, my sisters are standing up to these 'motherfuckers,' at the bus stop, at Aldi, in the parking lot, and you do it once, for five minutes, and you want to frame your certificate of participation on the wall."

"I don't think that's very fair."

"No, it's not. It's not fair."

And with that a silence fell over us, no one speaking again until a small sedan pulled up. "I'm sorry, I thought I ordered an XL," Birgit murmured. I volunteered to sit in the middle, finding myself sandwiched between the two feuding lovers, while Birgit took the front seat. We began our multi-stop route toward Dahlem, where thankfully I was to be the first drop-off, our tense, collective silence prompting the driver to scan the radio and settle on a distressing American pop song I recognized from the grocery stores.

"I fear for what's to come," Birgit said eventually. "I really do. I feel we are at the end of something. Or very close to the end."

"Of Berlin?" I asked, in jest, but Birgit did not smile. For her there was no joke, and her silence seemed to weigh the very city itself in the balance.

By mid-August the parched earth was hard and cracked, and the grass, now yellowed and crisp, stuck to our shoes like hay as we walked through it. Many of the regulars were already at the lake when we arrived, Evangeline in her Doc Martens and fluorescent-green tights, the same two families who set up camp by the fallen log, and of course the three Italians, all of whom I nodded to in greeting. The four of us were already sweating profusely as we took up our usual spot in the meadow. Disembodied screams and laughter from the lake echoed through the clearing, and Birgit contemplated taking a swim before it got any busier, to do her circuit around the perimeter before resting on the raft.

"From the sounds of it, there's already quite the crowd out there" Gabor said. "It'll be the Raft of Medusa soon enough."

"All right, all right, I'm going in," Birgit replied, removing her oversized shades, stripping naked, becoming herself a Paleolithic Venus, and ambling off toward the water. Eren and Gabor also undressed, Gabor's furred potbelly and ten-millimeter Prince Albert piercing catching the eyes of a nearby few as he reapplied sunscreen to his already-red face. We then sat together for a while, watching the new arrivals walking their bikes through the burnt grass, a man with a long, white braided beard like an old billy goat, an aging crust punk princess with a black head wrap, two lean French otters in matching yellow Speedos. Gabor took out a novel from his carrier bag, and opened it at the bookmark, but continued staring out across the meadow. For as long as I had known him he had been a distracted reader in public, scanning a few sentences before looking up again, seemingly incapable of tuning out nearby conversations, tutting and chuckling to himself periodically about the goings-on at a nearby blanket, and yet he always insisted on bringing the most demanding tomes to the lake, it was his most sadistic Hungarian trait. I lay back, resting my head against my knapsack, and, closing my eyes, I felt Lukas lie down beside me, the weight of his head on my chest, as we had rested so many times in that very spot.

The lake was the place where I felt I saw Lukas in his true form, not intoxicated, not in shadow, not posturing for the affections of others, the only place where his nakedness was not something for me to possess but something which belonged to nature alone. The final trip we ever made to Teufelssee together had also been one of the hottest days of the summer, humid and close without any relief, and as we lay together, Lukas told me he felt a kind of angered bewilderment at having a body but too few days left to truly understand and experience what that meant. It was only at Teufelssee, while sitting on the boulder by the cove watching me smile back at him from the water, that he felt time slow to the pace of thought, of breath, slow to the pace in which he might take notice of the variations in temperature between the direct and shaded sun, the ant with its crimson thorax that crawled below the arches of his arm hair, or the depth of his feeling for the man swimming toward him. How was it, he wondered, that a night at the bars could feel like a couple of hours, and an afternoon at Teufelssee could feel like a week, what was it that made time distort variously like light through thick glass? The boulder by the cove, a glacial erratic, belonging like the lake itself to deep time, once caught in the hot throat of the Earth before purged by fire, swept over mountains by retreating ice, and deposited there on the shore to be polished smooth by ten million nights of rain. This was the time to which Lukas and I now belonged together, a queer time, a time that defied the linear plotting of history as laid out by man like heads on pikes, not time as it has been hammered out like ore into a sword, but rather time that spread like a rhizome, with no discernible edge, no beginning or end, just a continual unfolding of interconnected experience, a bowl of water spilling in all directions at once, just as it was being constantly refilled by its own spilled water. I had, for the briefest of moments in my life, felt tangibly a part of this, felt time at once pouring from and filling me beyond myself.

I was stirred from my reverie by Birgit's return, and, squinting against the sun as I opened my eyes, gazed up at her toweling off above me.

"A vision to behold."

"It's heavenly," she said, beaming down at me.

I could hear Gabor rummaging in his carrier bag, and turned to see him holding a bar of psilocybin chocolate. Birgit knelt down beside us. "No, absolutely not."

"Oh, don't be such a narc," Gabor replied, breaking the small bar into four generous portions. I had taken mushrooms by the lake with Birgit and Gabor before, but Birgit expressed her uneasiness, given my current state. Gabor was of the exact opposite view, and had been encouraging me for days to take psilocybin for my depression and "death anxiety," as he called it. I sat up, and thanked Birgit for her concern, and tried to reassure her that a gentle midday trip was hardly going to push me over the edge, though her disapprobation persisted. I shared with them how, during one of my early digs in Grotte du Renne, we had found traces of gray shag mushroom in Neanderthal dental tartar, which delighted Gabor and Eren. The four of us spent the next several hours sitting together like a troop of saggy-titted gorillas, plucking from one another's heads jokes and stories and half-recalled gossip, encountering friends, laughing at the antics of strangers, and at times sitting in silence, reading and reapplying sunscreen to each other's backs. As the sun began its descending arc, I lay back to rest my head on my knapsack once more, and looking up I noticed the clouds appeared fractal, their edges filigreed, receding infinitely into smaller and finer swirls. Turning my head, I then gazed for a long while at the forest's edge, and I began to observe the movement of the wind articulating itself through every leaf, like applause. I looked down at my hand, resting in a patch of sunbaked earth, as a black-tailed skimmer with a powder-blue pruinescence on its abdomen landed beside it, and lingered for nearly a minute. In my stillness I became aware of the conversations unfolding on the blankets around me, and for a brief instant felt as if I could hear every conversation in the meadow at once. In my mind then appeared a word, an unsayable word, a word that did not exist, but was at the intersection of at least five other words, perhaps every word, the ur-word from which all sound, all color, all shapes emanated. I knew this word was where I was headed, the destination at the end of my life, I would arrive at this word, and I would be joined to it at long last, and when I did, all hidden meanings would be revealed. My attention slowly returned to the voices near me, Eren, Gabor, and Birgit talking, and I felt such deep love for them, this small family. We sat together until the sun passed below the tree line, and watched as the last of the evening bathers emerged from the water. Eren then shared that he and Gabor would not be making a visit to the forest that evening, as Gabor had torn his frenulum in an overly vigorous playdate. I expressed my sympathies, and kissed them goodbye, and though Birgit urged me to join them on their walk back to the S-Bahn, I calmly insisted that I wished to stay a little longer on my own, and that I would text them when I was safely home. I watched as the three receded from view through the meadow, glancing back more than once at me as they went.

I sat for a time, observing the nearby blanket of youths snorting lines of mephedrone and carrying on over a steady, thumping bass, before movement drew my eye toward the shore—a cerulean kingfisher swooping down and hovering for a moment just above the lake's surface, before aborting its kill and darting off. It was then that I noticed a figure standing in the silhouette of dusk by the water's edge, who I could swear had not been there a moment before. I shuddered and then sat immobilized, my eyes fixed on the dark form, half expecting him to disappear with my next blink. After a long while I rose, pulled on my clothes, folded my blanket into my bag, and descended the gradual slope toward the backlit man. Though his body was turned away from me, I knew it was Lukas long before I had reached him, just from his stance. The lake was now the same pearlescent blue as the black-tailed skimmer's abdomen, and undisturbed by any swimmer. As I arrived alongside Lukas, he turned to me and smiled, neither surprised nor perturbed by my presence. He wore the same knapsack he had always brought with him to the lake, invariably packed with books, a can of Crisco, and a bottle of poppers. Had some need of mine conjured him into being? Or was he merely a trick of the evening light? I glanced back at the youths in the meadow, but they remained oblivious to the quiet miracle unfolding on the shore. Not about to repeat my past mistake, with great stealth I removed my phone, opened the voice memo app, and pressed record, before returning it to my pocket. I somehow intuited that filming Lukas would be a step too far, a violation that might cause him to retreat or vanish altogether. I did not ask him, either, why he had come for me, from fear that doing so would tear the fragile membrane of reality in which we coexisted. As the forest's shadow claimed the last of the meadow, we walked together in silence back up the slope toward the footpath where, instead of taking my usual route home, Lukas turned northward. I walked with him through the evening's variegated light, our shoulders occasionally brushing, and watched as he picked up a stick and began slowly peeling it of its bark. At length, we found ourselves in a part of the forest where I rarely ventured, a graveyard of the nameless, with a low stone wall which I scaled with considerably more difficulty than Lukas, and we began to wander between the unmarked stones mantled with ivy, past the five Orthodox crosses with Cyrillic epitaphs honoring the Russian refugees loyal to Tsar Nicholas II who drowned themselves in the Havel after the October Revolution, and past the graves of sixty Berliners shot in the dying days of the Second World War, and past the listing, broken tombstones of babies too young to have been named. As night set in, we continued southward, the Havel at our backs, and as we walked I had the distinct impression that we were being watched, and though I knew if I were to turn around I would find no figures in the dark, I could not bear to look behind me no matter how much my rational mind willed it. We walked in the half-light past several forlorn wooden huts and an abandoned greenhouse, then through a great sandpit where several dogs with no apparent master chased each other barking. I had a thousand questions for Lukas, but with every footstep each one felt more irrelevant than the next, and eventually my mind emptied until I was nothing but in the unfolding present. I had the sense too that Lukas wanted to show me something, that he was guiding me not only to the cruising glades, but toward a secret knowledge he wished to impart. I followed him down a narrow path that wound its way through the underbrush in such serpentine fashion that I became disoriented, and for a while was sure we had doubled back on ourselves, but rather than reemerging at the sandpit, we stepped out into the clearing, beyond which I caught glimpses of bodies. We walked for several yards through the pines until we reached a fallen tree long stripped of its bark and smoothed by the elements, and I noticed two eight-inch knobs, about six feet apart, protruding from the silken trunk, each sanded down and rounded out. He watched the dawning realization and perturbation play across my face. I laughed, surely he was having me on, but he then reached into his knapsack and removed the Crisco. I felt the unsayable word on my lips as I pulled off my clothes, and, with a certain reluctant wonder, scooped up a handful of the grease and began lathering one of the knobs while Lukas did the same with the other. We then positioned ourselves as if facing each other on a great teeter-totter, and slowly lowered ourselves down onto the tree, gasping, and allowing ourselves to be filled by it. Never before had anything fit so perfectly, so completely, inside of me. I began to buck against the polished stump, holding Lukas's gaze and stroking my erection as if it were his, as if we were one body. I felt like a captive animal rewilded. With what intensity had I been domesticated? The answer lay in a space before memory. How feral might I really be? How many of us have allowed ourselves to truly know, and what must necessarily be destroyed in the search for that knowing? As I let the forest fuck me, I began to slip from the hook of myself, a dog in the sandpit, a seed spread on the wind, an untamed weed, I felt escaped, taken to the very brink of what my body could endure. I felt my awareness of all things around me sharpen, the seven million distinguishable colors of my human sight, the half million tones of my hearing, I was utterly permeable, with no distinction between my body, Lukas's, the earth, a moss-engorged log moldering back into the soil, every being that had ever nourished it with their body, the mystery was here all along, I had always been part of it, the immanence of all things, a raking light, lifting, alighting a lake a lack at last the moment in which we might rise and meet ourselves and know no there is no God heaven is here eternal life is what you are already part of you die you disperse what was you is reconstituted countless entities just as you have already been the pond the scum the sediment the dust in the light-shafts the gradual accretion of pollen spectra an ancient border of boreal birch phases pine phases larches spruce and alder phases the reeds the crane all time is in play all things unfolding at once every moment the same all of time pouring out and back into itself—

I admit, it was disturbing and ignoble to be discovered naked astride the log, and still very much joined to it. There was ejaculate on my hands, my chest, and across the log itself. I was unconscious, and slumped, head resting on my chest, and yet still upright, as if shot while riding a horse. I was shaken awake by two concerned strangers, two middle-aged men I recognized from the forest but with whom I had never exchanged words. As I returned at last to myself, and my eyes focused across the log, I realized Lukas was gone. The men were asking me questions, and one helped brace me as I gingerly lifted myself up off the stump, but I was distracted. I looked about for Lukas, but could find him nowhere. The tips of my fingers were cold, in fact I realized I had begun to shiver. I gathered up my pants, and from the left pocket pulled out my phone, and pressed stop on the audio recording. The recording was nearly five and a half hours long. How had so much time passed? It was then that I noticed the frantic text messages from Gabor and Birgit, and the eight missed calls. Before I had a chance to reply, I heard my own name called out in distress, as if from a search party. It was Gabor, and I cleared my throat and called back to him. His voice became excited, relieved, he kept calling my name as he drew closer, I could hear his approach through the underbrush, and at last he emerged from the shadows, storming toward me as the two strangers stepped aside in alarm.

"What the hell is wrong with you? Why haven't you called or replied—"

"I'm so sorry, I—"

"Is your phone dead?"

"No, it's—"

Gabor grabbed the phone from my hand, and it illuminated with his touch—"No! It's not even! Were you just ignoring us? Birgit's been beside herself, we thought something had happened to you, it's past midnight."

As the two men walked away, commiserating in German, I tried to explain to Gabor, with fumbling incoherence, that something had in fact happened, something I did not yet have words for. Possession? Transcendence? The forest had quite literally entered me.

"I saw Lukas, we walked together—" Gabor sighed, exasperated. "And I spoke with him, here, I even have proof, look, I—" I brought up the audio recording on my phone and pressed play. At first, all that could be heard was the sound of my fumbling fingers and the recorder being returned to my pocket. I skipped ahead, and heard only the sound of my feet crunching softly on the gravel path. Skipping ahead again, and again, one could hear nothing over the rustling of my phone against my jeans. It was only then that it occurred to me that perhaps Lukas and I really had never exchanged a single word, and yet so much had passed between us. "I promise you he was with me. And then I was not in my body, I was not even myself, I was—I don't know, I was completely dispersed." Gabor patiently helped dress me back into my clothes, and he walked with me out of the glade, and along the path where I had first met Lukas decades ago in a not-dissimilar state of distress, and we walked in a strained silence, like a parent and their child, until we reached the first public road, from which Gabor called a taxi and rode with me back to my flat. Gabor spoke with Birgit on the phone as I showered, and at the first light of dawn he kissed me good night, assured by my promises that I would get some rest.

Once alone, I searched my flat for some time and eventually found the field notebook that I had kept with me at Hohle Fels all those years ago, which still held the scent of the Ach's muddy banks, and from its crisped pages I plucked a photograph of Lukas and me from that summer, arms cast across each other's bare shoulders, light cascading down from the escarpment behind us. I could not remember who had taken the photograph, or how long it had been since I had last held it. I felt arrested anew by Lukas's casual virility, but also surprised, as if noticing for the first time the restive and oblivious beauty of my own youth. I then noticed another detail I hadn't before, the firm grip of Lukas's hand on my shoulder, compared to the looseness of my arm, my hand hanging limp over his collarbone. It was so legible now, how his need to hold on to me had always exceeded my need to hold on to him. To be held like that by Lukas—have I ever again known such purpose in my life? And yet at the time I did not even notice. I looked into his bright and lively eyes in the photograph, and felt him looking, through the lenses, through time, into mine, as if even then he was trying to tell my future self something of his want, his fear. Lukas knew, even then. I could see it in his grip.

How I would let him go. How he would die alone, unexpected, in the morning, while Birgit was out running errands and I was lecturing. What if I had held him tight until the end, and whispered my reassurance into his ear, as he had deserved? I wiped away the tears which had also taken me by surprise, but they came faster, heaved from me, I was gasping, the crying that outpaces breath, a drowning in oneself.

What persisted was the question of how to make sense of those hours with Lukas in the forest. There was, of course, the serious prospect that I had lost my mind. There was a sort of Christian-inflected interpretation that Lukas's soul, Sebastian's, Thomas's, perhaps dozens of other dead lovers of mine, were trapped in some kind of limbo at Teufelssee. But why? Were they emanations from the forest? Were they time travelers? Was I? More than perhaps most, I was curious about what certain cities looked like at different hours of the day in years before my birth, the scents of an Assyrian temple, the rituals of a Palaeolithic settlement, but if I could move through time with even a modest degree of will, I would invariably choose to spend time with the people I had loved, with whom my time had been cut short. This I now knew. What could I care about walking through the Hanging Gardens, when I could spend one more quiet hour in Lukas's arms? As Gabor and Eren cooked us dinner the following evening,

Birgit nodded sympathetically as I told her that I resisted explaining away the profound encounters of the summer to some tumor in my brain. Even imagining for a moment that these visions *were* brought on by the tumor, did that make the encounters any less real, any less revelatory? I told Birgit about what Lukas had revealed to me in the forest, how what had once terrified me about death, its finality, its impenetrability, was revealed to me to be its opposite, a continuity and porousness so total as to be indistinguishable from life. Her brow furrowed ever so slightly, and after a long moment she replied, "That was very generous of him." And I agreed with her. It was a grace beyond any I deserved.

"Do you think he knows?" she asked. "Is that why he's come back for you?"

"To prepare me?"

She shrugged, letting the possibility hang in the air between us. "What do you both think?" she asked, turning toward the kitchen as Eren lowered the heat on the reduction sauce and shared a glance with Gabor.

"What do I think? I think . . ." Eren struggled for words, and took a sip of wine. "It doesn't matter what I think, I don't think you should care."

"But I do," I said.

Eren exhaled slowly, put down his glass, and

seemed to study it for a moment. "I think you have been looking for magic, for miracles, for ghosts, so you have found them," he said, looking up at me. "You have fabricated them out of the stuff that life is simply made of—spotting a man who resembles your dead lover in a forest, a chance encounter with a friend the day before he dies, yes, some small wonders and coincidences, the story of some missing boy who is eventually found, but such is life. It is your perspective that is shifting, perhaps as you near death, I don't know, I don't mean to sound morbid, but from what I understand that can happen, we become more keenly aware, and everything becomes imbued with significance."

I weighed Eren's words in the silence that followed, and when it seemed no one would speak, I said at last, "Wouldn't it be lovely to have always lived our lives with such attentiveness?" Perhaps Eren was right, that as I moved closer toward death, I was becoming more attuned to the uneven stitching at the seams of the living and the nonliving planes, the temporal distortions caused by bodies moving through the world on either side of this divide, just as the surface of water is sometimes disturbed by fish as it is by boats.

The drought reached its apex in the third week of August. Rivers in Catalonia ebbed to the width of streams, exposing the eleventh-century church of Sant Romà de Sau, flooded up to its steeple in the sixties after the construction of a dam. A first-century Roman fort emerged on a dried riverbed in Galicia, a Palaeolithic stone circle reappeared in the central province Cáceres, and the remains of a bridge built by Nero were rediscovered along the silty bottom of the Tiber. Every pocket was turned out. Every unseen thing now visible. Ponds in the Grunewald became basins of cracked mud, and the younger trees browned to tinder. And I too found myself in a state of rapid depletion. A great fatigue began overtaking me by midday. An unsteadiness in the shower one evening was followed by episodes of alarming forgetfulness. A search for my house keys would have me circling my flat for nearly twenty minutes before I realized they were left hanging in the front door overnight.

I woke one afternoon to find an unexpected message in my inbox. One of the Janis Pfeiffers whom I had messaged weeks earlier had at long last written me back, but on opening his reply, I realized that it was in fact a message from this particular man's sister, Claudia. Her message was brief. She said that her brother Janis was, indeed, the man from the *Bild* article, that he had lived in Berlin until his death in 2017, and that she was open to discussing him with me should I still wish to. I called the phone number she included below her name, but after five rings it went to voicemail. At the sound of the tone, my nerves bested me, and I hung up without leaving a message. Instead, I sent her a text, in which I thanked her for her reply, and indicated my desire to speak at her nearest convenience. She texted back a few minutes later, and after a brief exchange suggested that the two of us meet at a Turkish coffee shop near her flat in Neukölln.

I arrived at the café at the appointed time of our meeting three days later, and though it was crowded, and I had no photo to go off of, as my eyes landed on a woman sitting at a table in the far corner near the toilets, I could immediately tell it was Claudia. She was in her mid-forties, slight, mousy brown hair, the skin of a chain-smoker, and wore a pink spaghetti-strap shirt that gave her the strange look of an aged teenager. She did not see me enter, and I stood for a moment observing her from a distance. There was a glass mug in her hands filled with mint leaves but emptied of tea, which suggested she had been sitting there for some time, though I had arrived five minutes early. As I walked toward her she looked up, and, meeting my eyes, proffered a perfunctory smile, and made no effort to stand, or shake my hand, as I pulled the chair out across from her and sat down in it. After some nervous small talk about the weather and the neighborhood, she thanked me for my initial message, and apologized for taking so long to write back. She said that her brother had struggled from severe mental health issues, and had lived with her in her flat for the last several years of his life. She did not specify how he died, but said that she maintained his Facebook page as a kind of online memorial, and periodically checked his inbox for messages. "He has one friend who still messages him, as if he were alive, even though this man knows that he's not. It's a strange kind of one-sided correspondence. I suppose he writes these messages for himself, but also, on some level, he writes them for me, knowing that I am reading them. I've never once replied, but I feel this strange kind of obligation to check every once in a while, so he sees that I've read them." A teenager with an upper lip faintly dusted with hair appeared at our table to take my order, and as he sullenly cleared our menus and walked away, Claudia asked me if I was a journalist.

"No. No, I'm an archaeologist. But my interest in your brother's story is—it's personal, not professional."

She nodded, though she seemed slightly more confused than before. I thought about telling her that I was a dying man. Perhaps she could already tell. She told me that I was the first stranger to reach out about Janis since the year of his reappearance, and that she had wrestled with herself for several days as to whether she would reply to me at all, but ultimately decided that talking about it might do her some good. I then asked her the indelicate but obvious question of how she was certain that the young man found naked at Teufelssee on the morning in 2009 was indeed her brother. She nodded, no doubt having asked this of herself numerous times before, and replied that, while she still had many questions about the mystery of her brother's disappearance, she never had a moment's doubt that the man was him.

"He had the same eyes, the same face, the same freckles on his shoulders. Even the same half smile. He had forgotten many of the names of our family, our grandparents, even our parents he wasn't so sure, but he remembered my name, and his best friend's name, a childhood friend. Trust me, he wasn't some fraud, he lived with me for years, it was him."

I nodded. I believed her more than I didn't. She looked down into her glass, as if trying to divine something from the sodden mint leaves. "Do I believe that he was somehow in the lake all of that time? No. Of course not."

"Then where do you think he was?"

I could tell this question unsettled her. She swallowed and looked back up at me.

"I think he was abducted. As a boy, when we were at the lake that day, with my mother. Probably by some kind of pedophile, some child molester. And then, I don't know . . . He had such trauma that his mind blanked out that time. Maybe it even induced some kind of psychosis, I don't know. But my guess is when he happened to return to Teufelssee as an adult, he suddenly remembered. He remembered who he had been before, he remembered my mother and me, and he—he came back to himself, it all came flooding back."

The waiter returned with my coffee and, sensing the moment he was interrupting, placed it in front of me without eye contact or uttering a word. Claudia's elbows were now both on the table as she held her hands balled up in front of her mouth and stared off to the side into the middle distance, before returning her eyes to mine. "When we reunited, I urged him to seek therapy. I basically forced him a couple of times. But. He was very damaged, I think. He didn't want to go. It was painful for him, and confusing." Her gaze wandered up to the Turkish music videos playing on a television mounted above the bar. "In many ways I prefer his version of the story," she said, turning back to me, and lowering her hands to reveal a hesitant smile. She told me that for all of the years Janis was missing, she had not been able to set foot in the Grunewald, but after his return, she had gone with him once to Teufelssee, to see if being at the lake prompted any further memories. It had not.

"But I do think there is something about that place. I can't quite say, really. Just a feeling I get when I'm there." She shook her head, her gaze distant. "They used to make human sacrifices there, did you know that?"

"Who did?"

"The pagans, a long time ago."

"No, I didn't know that."

"Well, you should, you're the archaeologist."

"You're right," I said, smiling.

"That's why it's called Devil's Lake. I remember reading in school about the warring tribes, and how they would lead prisoners of war into the grove with their hands chained, and the priestesses would crown them with wreaths and then take them to this raised platform and cut their throats, and from the blood that poured onto the ground they would make a prophecy. And other times, they would split open the body, and would make prophecies from the—what would you call it, the intestines, basically." She said the high priestess would then perform a ritual to open the unseen doors of the afterlife, so that the living and the dead might pass freely between. "I think that kind of thing, over a long time, it does something to a place. But also there was obviously already something about that forest, and that lake, that drew them to that spot specifically, don't you think? I don't think people come back to a spot, over and over, for no reason."

I told her that I had been thinking about this very thing, in some manner, all summer. It was the reason for my interest in her brother's story. I considered sharing with her my experiences, but I could think of no way to do so without leaving her in doubt of my sanity. Her comment made me wonder, though, whether there were certain places on Earth where the membrane between the past and present, indeed even the future, had been worn thinner than elsewhere. Whether people across cultures, throughout history, had been able to perceive this thinness, both consciously and unconsciously, and if it was because of this that these sites became places of worship, or at the very least places of congregation. Places where we return over and over to be with time, to better perceive its flux, and situate ourselves within its mysteries.

On what must have been our last visit to Teufelssee together I was standing in the clearing when I saw Lukas emerge from down a path, walking toward me with a big grin, and I expected him to start bragging about some gag-reflex-defying conquest he had just managed, but instead he told me that he felt dizzy, a bit weak, and had rested on a fallen tree for a moment, and as he did he had closed his eyes and experienced something strange that he could not quite put into words, perhaps he had drifted into sleep or slipped into that fragile state between waking and dreaming, but he said that as he rested there he glimpsed a secret, a vision, of what happens next, he felt he became a great many people, both living and dead, and though he did not fully understand what he had seen, he was no longer afraid. He no longer feared death. I could neither believe nor comprehend what Lukas was saying and assumed that he must be having some kind of hallucination, perhaps some reaction to the change in his medication. In truth, what I could not comprehend at the time was being unafraid of death, though I do know now what he glimpsed in those woods, for I have seen it too.

"I think we should get married."

"What?"

"Hear me out, I've been thinking about it—"

Birgit put her hand over my glass of wine. "I'm cutting you off."

"No, listen to me, I'm serious. You have always taken care of us, of me, and now it's my time to take care of you, to make sure you never have to worry again about stretching your pension or taking a vacation, I want you to do the things that you haven't let yourself do, please just—just listen. I have the cottage in Cornwall, all right, I have some savings. If we were married, you wouldn't have to pay any inheritance tax, and you'd have the benefit of my pension. I could leave you the cottage, you could rent it out in the summers too, then go up and write there in the fall, or sell it if you want, you'd have half of my savings, the other half would go to Gabor. I know this is hardly very sentimental or romantic, but I don't want anything so morbid as a funeral, all right, but a wedding, see *that* is an occasion to celebrate and dress up for."

Birgit wiped her eyes with two fingers while chuckling. "You're fucking ridiculous, you know that."

"I think it would be nice, a late August wedding."

"Late August? So this is a shotgun wedding?"

"Yes, I'm pregnant, in case you haven't heard."

"Oh really?"

"Yes, I have a little fetus growing in my head."

"Well. Then. I guess we should start planning."

Birgit held my gaze, the smile slowly disappearing from her face as she considered in earnest what I was proposing. She reached out and took hold of my hand, and we began to laugh, and she forbade me to cry, though could not hold herself to the same standard.

As we sat at my kitchen table, we began to talk this fantasy into being, how we would hold the ceremony in the evening by the lake, and we would ask Jana to be our officiant, for she was always calm and clear with her words, and we began drawing up a list of invitees, we wanted to keep it intimate, and of course it had to be people who were in town, and who could make it with little notice.

"Should it be casual, or should people dress up?"

"Of course they should dress up, it's our wedding."

"Okay, so formal—"

"Not *formal*, but dress-up."

"*Verkleiden*."

"Yes, exactly," I said with a giggle.

"You say *verkleiden* and they're going to think *Eyes Wide Shut*."

"Yes, why not, tell them to bring their masks. Eren can bring his leather hood."

Gabor and Eren naturally rallied, and insisted on cooking all of the food, and supplying the alcohol, for there had to be nice wine, and they also took on all the logistics, the transportation, blankets, pillows, coolers, serving dishes. I told them I didn't want it to get out of hand, no chairs and tables, no decorations, just ten to fifteen friends, and that was what it was. We stood on the shore at Teufelssee at sunset, Birgit in a simple blue dress, me in navy slacks and a matching blazer, hardly groundbreaking, but fetching, Antje between us, guiding the ceremony as our friends stood in a staggered semicircle in their summer suits, and gowns, and in a few cases T-shirts, shorts, and sandals. Antje spoke of the unbreakable bonds of friendship, love on the precipice of transformation, and of the unknown journey ahead, as all the while bemused onlookers watched from their blankets, children cannonballed from the pontoon raft, and a great undersong thrummed from the battling speakers across the meadow. It had been one of the hottest days of the summer, though as Antje's blessings drew to a close, a shadow passed over us, and a cool breeze blew through the grass, and looking up I suddenly noticed cumulonimbus clouds towering high into the stratosphere, heavy and gray, which I could have sworn had not been there even five minutes earlier. I saw the first drops of rain on the lake before I began to feel them atop my head, and then upon my face, and then the skies opened, and the parched earth drank as the wedding party squealed and laughed and ran for the cover of the nearby forest, but our suits and dresses were already sodden, the lake now a ferocious mist, there was no middle ground or distance, just wet bodies huddling and shivering below sheltering boughs, wiping their smiling faces, and speaking to each other in four human languages. It seemed silly to speak of good luck and fortune at a wedding like this, and yet we did, we could not help ourselves. We abandoned thoughts of returning to the lake as even our socks became wet in our shoes, and so we all moved deeper into the forest, which even at its densest offered only partial cover. I held Birgit's hands as she pulled off her shoes, and she held mine as I did the same. The sky had darkened into a strange twilight, and our white shirts clung to our bodies, joyful wraiths stumbling over roots and the uneven ground with yips and shrieks, our feet sponging into the sodden mat of pine needles. Mist rose from the earth. A moss, previously invisible when desiccated brown, turned a brilliant teal on the backs of all the quenched trees. Everything was awake in the living realm.

Birgit suddenly came up short in front of me, and I stopped behind her, her eyes trained on something ahead of her in the undergrowth. "Look," she whispered, with quiet wonder. "Do you see her?"

I scanned the darkness, over and over, but I could not see. "Right there! Right in front of you." And then at last I did. Standing not more than ten feet from us amid the bracken and ferns, with her gleaming eyes and bristled snout, was Elsa. The white of her face and black of her ears always distinguished her from the others. She was wet and alone, where were her piglets I wondered, surely they were not already old enough to fend for themselves. Gabor and Eren ar-

ORPHAN HOLD
DO NOT SHIP

H1 – 000000000407

ISBN 9780008794552

CLIENT Alternate Sourcing
STATION TPP Receiving Station 03
HELD 2026 – 10 – 08 14:18

SHELF

If its order arrives, scan this label at a receiving station.

rived behind Birgit and me, placing their hands on our shoulders, and, looking in the direction of our gaze, eventually saw Elsa as well. The pig whose life we had all spared, each of us in our way. We stood as quietly and still as possible, not wanting to startle her, as the rest of the wedding party continued onward, their voices receding. What did she make of us, I wondered, these specters who drifted in and out of her life, and exerted so much distant control over it, in ways she could scarcely fathom though perhaps intuited? Did she have another summer in her? Would she return to this forest, to Teufelssee, after I was gone? Where were her brood, I wondered again, had she somehow lost them, was she grieving, had she ever felt anything toward them that resembled love, love as I had known it, or rather, had my longing ever resembled any feeling she had known, and did it reside in her body as it did in mine like a physical sensation, a pressure, a threshing, a blade, or was it instinct, a pull in the blood, a searching and never finding? I looked into the infinity of her small eyes, all pupil, as she stared back into mine. What had my search revealed? If I was no longer afraid of death, was I no longer animal, no longer human, was I a revenant, then, caught between worlds, if there was even any distinction to be made between worlds? I am trying to tell you something beyond language. Then speak to me, I replied. Tell me what you know, and I will tell you what I know. It lives inside of you already. You have glimpsed the other side of the mirror and seen your own hand holding it. On the other side of the mirror is a mirror, just as the other side of your hand is your hand, and it may turn in either direction. I am all hunger, roots, bulbs, seedlings, wild garlic in the spring, especially after a long rain, sweet woodruff in moist shaded spots, earthworms, slugs, centipedes, moles, I'll eat bird eggs if I can get them, who wouldn't, only a couple of times in my whole life though, a nest has to fall or an egg from a nest, it's a rare treat to arrive at first, white asparagus, dandelions, though often too bitter, lizards, snakes, hard to chase, fish, hard too, frogs, hard, I'll take carrion of any kind, but all of that in the summer mostly, when everything is easy, and the sun moves us into motion, the heat of my fur, the warm mud stuck in my hooves, and when the visitors return and leave their food out in the grass, scattered, and wrapped, and scream at us back into the trees, clapping, it's a strange kind of game with them, we will come back, as often as they do, we will wait, as we've been taught, while they do as they've been taught, but their season is short, as the days shorten the meadow empties, and that's when I love it best, the mushrooms and hazelnuts, and will dig down to find more on the cold nights, through the frost, through the snow when it comes, and when the hard ground begins to soften again it's rutting season, and my brothers leave, with the yellow foam of their testicles, but I stay with our mother, or we would lose territory, all the gains we fought so hard for, the grazing grounds, along the lake and up the slope, someone has to stay and keep guard, as the roaming males start arriving hard-armored and vicious, they drive off my brothers, and chase us, to exhaust and overtake us, and take six, seven, eight of us in a rut, we maul and gouge them, and bite their penises, I would rip their penises clean off if I could, and try to, we don't give ourselves up without blood, but this is the cruel cycle from which we have all come, it takes and I find myself laden with life, heavy and slow, and a deep hunger renews itself with spring, farrowing, I carry six piglets inside of me, whom I birth when I feel the first heat of sunlight on my face after the long winter, whelped into a nest I've made in the tall grasses with sticks and leaves, my sisters around me, my mother, the six of them wrapped in my slickness, their color and scent already familiar, a part of my own, just the sound of them, what it stirs, a wild instinct, their bare, pink bellies, and two little milk teeth to latch and suck down either side of me, I feel overcome at times, not enough of me, enough space, air to breath, as each one fights harder than the next, growing faster, stronger, as they drain me of every drop of myself, until I grow too hungry, and shake free, and set out for food, they cluster tightly, pressed for warmth, and when I return, we all retake our positions, and the feeding resumes, soon all of us sated, hidden in our warm clutch, but in time we all emerge, they walk with me, through the shimmer and cool, in the rain, and through the dark, I show them what to eat and what not, when to run and when to stay still, their colors change, their teeth, they defy me, in the meadow, in the heat, they get themselves plugged into a cake, devouring it, screaming and caking on the children, whipping everything up, a frenzy, almost proud of it, but there's something dangerous, no, no, don't let them touch you, a danger, yes, as they begin to clap at us, and whistle and clap hard, and shout, okay we turn, we go back, follow me, quick now, we go back, cake-snouted, it was fun while it lasted I admit, but then the rain doesn't come again, not all summer, just dust and heat and nothing to eat but garbage, I see a young suckling die, not mine, but we eat it, we have no choice, we are dying, and the heat drives us mad, and I grow weary, slowly, even as my children grow fast, and beyond me, and yet somehow remain always a part of me, this I learn, even at a distance, in absence, and then at last the cool nights come again, and the rain, and the males come again from elsewhere, they always do, I remember some of them, their brutal faces, their scents, again we draw blood, spattered across the snow, and again I find myself weighted with new life, everything resets, just as my sons grow impatient, their testicles double and frothing, go off to fresh mayhem, to do what has been done to me, their sisters, infinite life, infinite, insistent life, though blood must always be shed, I think of them, though less each day, find myself slower this season, slow through the cold, lesions on my lower jaw, and in my lungs a heavy blood rot, coughing, I'd seen it on the strange males, black tusk, open wound, they brought this death with them, though death is in all things, I have always known this, worms, ticks, blood-sucking flies, the soft mammal, you learn this with time, death is insistent too, infinite, I have carried so much, and this great exhaustion comes over me slowly, a slow down heavy rot that takes me down into the cold one night, and from which I do not rise, and with my daughters around me, nudging their snouts, and warming me, I do not rise from the darkness, not this time, not ever.

It was not so long away, the end. I could already feel the evenings trailing off into the first mumblings of autumn. Even a summer cannot last. At the age of four I discovered I could slow time to the point of almost total atrophy by sitting in a hot corner of dusty sunlight.

I learned, with enough patience, time could become transformed from a condition into a material, something one could hold, and bend. In this way, there was no time, only place. Only Birgit, Gabor, and Eren watching the gradations of late afternoon light over the lake as they sat in our usual spot in the meadow. By their side, I was now entirely contained within the confines of a plastic sandwich bag. Discrete and portable. Carried to the lake in Birgit's knapsack. They waited until sunset, when only a handful of bathers remained. Songs and poems were discussed, but in the end, they opted for silence. To spread slowly over the surface of Teufelssee is to never again have to justify my nature, to never again regret missing the train, or the low tide, to over-pour the wineglass and leave a ring around its base, to lie in the grass and feel a skyscraper tumbling toward me from the quick passage of clouds beyond it, the apricot light over a dead November field, the iridescent morning shifting across frozen prisms of ice on a glass door, the white-blue arch-weld through your eyelids, the dog whose whimper sounds like a wet cloth wiping a mirror, to spread slowly over the surface, poured out into the water that is forever pouring out of me, glacial meltwater warmed by the last of the August light, as it is every year, century after century, is to never again apologize for absence, or presence, or physical failings, culinary failings, failings of belief, is to never again hold a grudge, a secret, an erection, a glass of Sancerre, your hand. If only I could truly speak to you of this lake this portal this sky-mirror if only I could account for every detail to tell you of the kingfisher and the stork the ants with their red thoraxes the man with his thick tawny viking beard buttocks of white marble in repose sylphlike along the shore his lover with geometric tattoos tracing his spine they dash in splashing a diamond net cast glinting as minnows trace my toes in the cove my God the ten white buoys dotting the perimeter the fallen trees beyond half submerged along the far side where an elderly man carves a languid front crawl alongside a watchful mother duck and her brood if I could tell you of the most intense golden light that starts around five and continues until the forest's shadow overtakes the shrieking laughter of children disembodied and echoing like cave paintings the shiver of a weed caressing my ankle as I swim like the dead reaching up for me but not yet I whisper not yet as somewhere below me my watch still counts the seconds minutes hours of my life in the darkness.

ACKNOWLEDGMENTS

Thank you to Kishani Widyaratna at 4th Estate, Jackson Howard and Eliza Rudalevige at FSG, Jennifer Lambert at HarperCollins Canada, Jane Finigan, Molly Glick, Imogen Sarre, John MacGregor, Alistair Wroe, Ben Miller, Brandon Flynn, the dogs, and the pigs.